Acclaim For the
MAX ALLA

"Crime fiction aficionados are in for a treat...a neo-pulp noir classic."
> —*Chicago Tribune*

"No one can twist you through a maze with as much intensity and suspense as Max Allan Collins."
> —*Clive Cussler*

"Collins never misses a beat...All the stand-up pleasures of dime-store pulp with no cut-rate complexity."
> —*Booklist*

"Collins has an outwardly artless style that conceals a great deal of art."
> —*New York Times Book Review*

"Max Allan Collins is the closest thing we have to a 21st-century Mickey Spillane and...will please any fan of old-school, hardboiled crime fiction."
> —*This Week*

"A suspenseful, wild night's ride [from] one of the finest writers of crime fiction that the U.S. has produced."
> —*Book Reporter*

"This book is about as perfect a page turner as you'll find."
> —*Library Journal*

"Bristling with suspense and sexuality, this book is a welcome addition to the Hard Case Crime library."
> —*Publishers Weekly*

They got dressed for their night out—the reservation at Hugo's Cellar was for eight—with Nolan in his milk-chocolate Armani suit and Sherry in a black evening gown with gold filigree at the shoulders, a bare back and a side slit.

Goddamnit, he loved this woman. He'd let himself love a woman once, a long time ago, and then she got herself killed, and he swore off such foolishness. But his life was different now. He wasn't some hard guy thief anymore, was he? He'd tried explaining it to Jon.

Nolan was strictly legit these days, with a beautiful young wife—some might call her a trophy wife...well, the hell with them. He loved her. From the ground up, from the hair down.

Life was good now.

They were just preparing to go out for their evening at one of the best restaurants in Las Vegas, where an old friend and his wife would be waiting, when the men in ski masks and guns burst in....

Skim
DEEP

by **Max Allan Collins**

A HARD CASE CRIME NOVEL

A HARD CASE CRIME BOOK
(HCC-146)
First Hard Case Crime edition: November 2020

Published by

Titan Books
A division of Titan Publishing Group Ltd
144 Southwark Street
London SE1 0UP

in collaboration with Winterfall LLC

Print edition ISBN 978-1-78909-139-7
E-book ISBN 978-1-78909-140-3

Design direction by Max Phillips
www.maxphillips.net

Typeset by Swordsmith Productions

Printed and bound by CPI Group (UK) Ltd, Croydon CR0 4YY

Visit us on the web at www.HardCaseCrime.com

For every one of you
who has been here
since **BAIT MONEY**

Las Vegas is the only place I know
where money really talks.
It says, "Goodbye."
FRANK SINATRA

Money—the one lubrication for love.
CHESTER HIMES

AUTHOR'S NOTE

As is the case with the Quarry novels I've written for my friend
Charles Ardai at Hard Case Crime, this book stays within the original
time frame of the Nolan series. I consider it a novel written in period,
not a historical novel, though I doubt that distinction matters to
anyone but me.

The action here takes place six months or so after *Spree* (1987—
to be republished by HCC as *Mad Money*).

As my dedication indicates, I am grateful to longtime readers
who have been after me for some while to tell more of Nolan and
Jon's story (and Sherry's). I am also grateful to the late Donald E.
Westlake (aka Richard Stark) for allowing me to turn a novel that
had been intended as a one-time homage (*Bait Money*, 1973, republished by HCC as half of *Two for the Money*), into a full-blown
series. As I reminded Don many times, "homage" is French for
"rip-off."

But we're all thieves here.

SKIM DEEP

ONE

Cole Comfort, being dead, no longer lived in his rustic house in the country outside Jefferson City, Missouri. He lived nowhere, obviously, though what was left of him had been buried near Davenport, Iowa, in a gully where the ground was soft enough to dig deep but not so close to the little stream as to get exposed, if the water overran.

He lived on in the memory of his mother, though the location of Cole's earthly remains—in fact, even whether he truly had died—was unknown to her. Not that she had any doubt that her boy, missing six months, was dead at the hands of a ruthless son of a bitch named Nolan.

Mabel Winifred Comfort, known to one and all as Maw, lived in her son's humble, plunder-filled farmhouse, a turn-of-the-century structure wearing aluminum siding the way a thief does a stocking mask. She appeared harmless enough, an old lady, overweight, struggling around the place with her walker, the upstairs of the two-story house a country she could no longer visit.

Thanks to the choppers Coleman bought her, Maw still had the lovely smile whose sadistic aspect escaped notice of some, often to their peril. She had been lovely herself once, a show-girl in Kansas City in her teens, a high-class hooker in St. Lou in her twenties, and then the devoted mother of three boys—Samuel, Coleman, and Daniel.

Their father, Jedidiah, had been gone so long, his face was a blur to her. The only picture she had of him was from a wanted poster and that was faded with age worse than she was. Had it really been fifty-year or more that Jed wooed her back with him to the hardscrabble Georgia sticks that spawned him?

Some gangsters Jed crossed in the Lou had been after him, but in time the law and rival hoods took care of that, and finally the Comforts wound up back in the Show Me State. He'd always been a good provider, Jed, and he died brave, exchanging gunfire with a grocer.

Maw was likely in her seventies somewheres, but in those days in backwoods Missouri, such inconsequential things as getting born weren't well kept track of. Her girlish figure had long since become a memory under a succession of colorful muumuus, floral mostly; what had once jiggled now undulated like water about to come to a boil. Short sexy curls were a now frizzy gray skullcap.

For years she had lived with Coleman and his son and daughter—dumb-as-a-stump Lyle and jailbait babydoll Cindy Lou. Six months ago the boy's butchered body turned up in a ditch a few miles from this house, and the girl was off in Hollywood making dirty movies, if family gossip was to be believed. To Maw that was a step up from just giving it away.

What blew things to hell and gone was Coleman's scheme to blackmail former accomplice Nolan into helping loot a big shopping mall in Davenport, Iowa. In a nursing home at the time, Maw was only on the fringes of the thing; but Cole had spoke to her about it, grinning that grin so much like hers, proud of what he was cooking up. Such a handsome boy with that snow-white hair, full head of it, too. He'd been visiting her at Sunny Acres, an assisted care facility in Jefferson City.

She'd not been a resident, though, just recovering there from hip surgery, having taken a fall in the parking lot outside the Golden Spike Bar & Grill. Cole had bought her a new hip, a plastic one. That was just the kind of son he was, even if she sometimes cursed him for that hip, when it rained bad and got sore as a boil.

Why didn't you just let me die, you dumb son of a bitch? she would say even now. But then she'd smile to herself, thinking how much she loved him.

How much she missed him.

She knew that bastard Nolan, who years ago had done a few jobs with Sam and Cole, had killed her firstborn and now likely her middle boy, too. Cole's mall score didn't come off and everybody connected with it either run for the hills or was dead. In the aftermath, somebody had killed Lyle, likely right here in this house when he got back home, judging by the blood spatter left behind like a grisly "fuck you." Probably that was Nolan, too. Nothing worse than a goddamned reformed crook.

Mabel Winifred Comfort wanted nothing else out of this life but resolution of what was done to Coleman. Well, resolution and continued comfort. She ate well, having groceries delivered, and she ordered off Home Shopping Network all kinds of goodies, beauty products and exercise machines and jewelry, most of which remained in their boxes, stacked in the downstairs spare bedroom.

Her barn was filled with boxes, too, of such items as microwave ovens and VCRs and TVs, from tiny to big, and cigarettes and booze and various other things and stuff that made life worth living, or at least ways tolerable. These were items she bought, but not from Home Shopping. Maw had taken over her late son Coleman's fencing operation, buying and selling, dealing only in cold hard cash. Jars and shoeboxes of the stuff were squirreled around the place, which was hers now, not that any deed said so.

Daniel had moved her in, maybe a month after Coleman

disappeared off the face of God's good earth. She hadn't seen him since, though it was only a two-hour drive. He did talk to her on the phone once a month. Big of him.

Always a disappointment to her, Daniel—at 45, the youngest—was kind of a black sheep, or maybe in the Comfort family more a white one. He'd got himself some kind of two-year degree in accounting from a junior college and then a job as a bank teller. He weaseled his way up, over the years, to loan officer in a bank in O'Fallon, a suburb of St. Lou.

And he never *once* used that position to help Cole or any of the Comforts rob the goddamn fuckin' place! What kind of boy had she raised anyway? Did the wolves switch her baby for a lamb? He didn't even use the name Comfort! He was Daniel Clifford, legally.

It was like he was ashamed of his own kin! Of course the Comforts had made the papers in Missouri, over the years time to time, and that might be the why. Benefit of the doubt.

She kept the place tidy, or rather the colored girl who came in once a month did—that gal was about due, because right now the kitchen sink and counter were piled high with dirty dishes and this and that. Till the cleaning gal come in, Maw couldn't cook anything but TV dinners, like the Hungry Man turkey and fixings she put away at noon.

But Maw liked keeping a nice house. She had to put up with leaving it crummy outside. The two-story was set back off a gravel road that cut through farmland the family hadn't owned for ages, with a sagging silo and an overgrown yard home to various dead vehicles that were rusting into art pieces....

It all seemed an unlikely setting for a fencing operation that brought in thousands every week. She had a boy from town (who'd worked with Cole) who came by to supervise the unloading of merchandise into the barn or up on the second floor.

The first floor of the farmhouse was pretty much her whole world. She had struggled with the interior decorating. Other than her own bedroom, she'd never had any input in that regard—and she was okay with that. It had been Coleman's house to live in as he chose with his boy and girl. If he wanted velvet paintings of John Wayne and Elvis all over the cheaply woodgrain-paneled living room walls, that was his right; she had her kitten posters and her frog collection in her own quarters to suit her.

With Coleman likely passed, she might have taken those Elvises down, skinny and fat alike, and the old and young Duke, too. Only she just couldn't bring herself. They weren't to her more refined tastes, true, but they were Coleman. They represented him. They made it feel like he was still here, like the smell of his cigar smoke that was still in the drapes.

Nothing wrong with the furniture in that living room, though. No, Coleman had seen to it that they had only the best, and at Maw's request kept the couches and recliners and such protected in clear vinyl. She might have preferred just early American, and not this mix of modern and traditional and every other damn style you could think of. But that reflected less what Coleman's personal preference was and more what had been in the furniture warehouse he looted that time.

One favor she meant to have Daniel do her was deal with all that stereo equipment. It didn't play her collection of Red Foley, Little Jimmy and Ernest Tubb 45 EPs and 33 1/3 LP albums. She had hundreds of 78's, too, and nothing to spin them on! That fucking thing in the living room took only those little silver discs. Her last surviving son would do her one favor, anyway—*get her a goddamned record player!*

Daniel could have the rest of the stereo stuff. She'd considered selling it, but her fencing operation dealt in strictly new, in-the-box merchandise—that was what the clientele Coleman bequeathed to her required.

She had another favor from Daniel in mind, too. Which truth be told was even more important than finding a way to play her Porter Wagoner records. And he was coming, Daniel was, this afternoon. He'd called all soft-spoken but the anxiety showed through. Wanted to talk to her. She could guess what about, and it made her smile, those choppers gleaming at her in her reflection as she sat across from the Budweiser mirror by the big-screen TV, leaning back in her recliner, the only one not covered in plastic, since she didn't like the way her big fat butt made it squeak.

Goddamn, to be young again.

What was left to an old woman but comfort and resolution? And of course by resolution what she meant was restitution. And what she meant by restitution was revenge. Good old fashioned eye-for-an-eye type revenge, although that wasn't enough. Not near enough. Two eyes for one, maybe. Three. She'd come up with something.

Besides making money from stolen goods, and ordering things from Home Shopping that she (and, really, nobody) didn't need, Maw had two hobbies.

One was collecting Precious Moments figurines. The only addition she had made to the living room decor, otherwise a kind of shrine to her late son Coleman, were several mounted multi-tiered shelves of the little pastel children and their pets, many of the kiddies cast as angels and Biblical prophets. She had all the "Original 21" figurines—her favorite was "God Loveth a Cheerful Giver," a sweet little girl giving away puppies from a wooden cart. For her birthday three years ago, Coleman took her to the Precious Moments theme park, with its chapel, in Carthage, a three-hour drive.

That was the kind of son Coleman had been.

Her other hobby, picked up many years ago the way some gals pick up knitting, was basket weaving. It relaxed her. Soothed her. Mellowed her out. Kept her from hitting the sauce too hard, because you needed a clear head and steady hands.

And her hands were steady, all right. She had bad knees and arthritis in the hip area, but her hands were fine, just fine. She had a table set up in what had been Cindy Lou's bedroom where she could work with sturdy scissors and her sharp knife, side cutters too, for chipping off ends. Round-nosed pliers to kink the stakes before bending—she liked the angles nice and sharp. She'd paid good money for her bodkin, the wooden-handled pointed tool that made spaces between woven work, and could push a rod into position where a gap had been fashioned.

While mourning Coleman, she'd got carried away some, buying yard after yard of natural reed, weaving up a storm, doing her own staining and dyeing. Cole's bed was covered with baskets, stacks of them, all sizes and various shapes. She'd done some of those at Sunny Acres. Country Crafts, a gift shop in Jefferson City, handled some of her baskets on consignment, but she had more than they could take on at the moment.

Maw used her walker to convey herself into the bathroom, where she freshened up. Put on lipstick and some powder. She wanted to look good for her son. It was important to her that Daniel knew she was still in the game. Not some old biddy, but a player. Her face was smooth, except around her mouth, where vertical lines left the telltale marks of the longtime smoker. She'd stopped ten years ago—or was it eleven?—when a doctor said he couldn't find a pulse in her legs.

Nonetheless, she hated the face that looked back at her in that goddamned mirror. She had been beautiful once. Men had paid good money to slide their dicks in that red mouth, and her lower lips, too; but she never let them plow her back garden. She was just not that kind of girl.

Maw and her walker trudged into the kitchen, where she cleared the table, somehow squeezing more things onto the counter, and readied for her son. She set a bowl of Spanish peanuts out. An ashtray too, because he still smoked. Cans of Bud were cooling in the fridge. More fuss than that he did not deserve.

Gravel stirred outside, as a car pulled from the road into the drive. She and the walker waddled back into the living room, and she used the remote on her recliner arm to turn down the big-screen TV on Home Shopping, where Marie Osmond was selling a Marie Osmond doll, and got the front door open. Her youngest son's car was a Buick Skylark, light tan with a darker brown vinyl top. He parked behind a baby blue Cadillac Coupe DeVille that Coleman had bought her—that was the kind of son Coleman was. Driving was a bitch after the hip replacement, though, so mostly it just sat.

Daniel got out of the Buick and into the sunny June afternoon, cool for this time of year. He wore sunglasses, a small man with a skimpy mustache and thinning dark hair and an oval face whose shape and sharp features reminded her of a long dead aunt she'd never liked.

He lifted a hello hand as if it were heavy and his smile seemed to take effort, too. His polo shirt was V-neck and white, his slacks gray, his tasseled shoes white leather; he was sockless. This was part of his attempt to look young for that new wife of his. His third.

The first had been nice, a plain girl with flat features and a flat chest but a loving little thing until she divorced him over the second girl, who was also plain but not flat-chested. After that one ran around on him, Daniel was single for a while and took to bar-crawling, as Cole described it, and had a year or so ago married the recent one, who was in her twenties and cute and also not flat-chested but a little fucking gold digger. Also Cole's words.

Coleman had always considered Daniel a disgrace and a goddamned embarrassment to the family. And she couldn't say he'd been wrong.

Daniel navigated the dead vehicles and made his way up the cement stoop to the open front door and stood there like a trick or treater, just looking at her.

"Maw," he said.

"Daniel," she said.

She scooched back some with her walker, motioned him in, and soon they were sitting at the kitchen table with beer and peanuts and exchanging a few pleasantries.

Strange not having Cole here, Maw. It is. *You need to get to know Heather, Maw. You'd like her if you knew her better.* Bring her by. *I finally got over that cold.* Good to hear. *Can you believe Bill is in high school now?* Right age for it.

Bill, her only grandchild by Daniel, was by the first plain wife, who raised the child. Maw didn't know the boy well. She did know he'd been a smart aleck who could've used a firmer hand. Sprout could have used some time with the Good Book, which is what Maw and her late husband had slapped and whipped their brood with when a lesson needed learning.

"Mind if I smoke, Maw?"

"Please. Other people's is all I get these days."

He dug the pack from his breast pocket, which had an alligator on it. "I'm glad you gave it up. They say it can kill you."

"That's the rumor."

He lighted up a Kent, got it going, then sat there staring past her, getting his nerve up.

She asked, "How much?"

He blinked at her. "What?"

"How much does she want?"

"How much does who want?"

Maw sipped at her can of Bud. "Heather. Enough for her own car? Maybe just a new one. That Buick's five years old if it's a day."

He shook his head. "Nothing to do with Heather. Not… directly."

She nibbled a couple of peanuts. "What, then?"

"I got myself in trouble."

"With another woman? Pregnant you mean, or just cheating?"

His blue eyes, the only thing about him like Cole, popped at her. "No! I'm a one-woman man, Maw, you know that."

One woman at a time, she thought.

She said, "Just spit it out, then."

"I borrowed some money."

"Where from? Your bank?"

"Yes."

She unleashed the grin. "You mean you got your hand in the till, boy?"

He swallowed; it made the excuse for a mustache twitch. Sighed. Nodded.

"I know a shylock," she said, with a shrug, tossing back some peanuts.

"No time for that. Anyway, I'd only get in deeper."

"Didn't know you had it in you. Took you long enough. Make me proud, if you weren't such a sniveling little girl about it."

He was staring into the ashtray. "We bought a new house."

"Don't remember bein' invited to the housewarming. Overspend, did you?"

He nodded. "I paid off the contractor. We can make the

monthly payments, no problem. But there were cost overruns, and...anyway. I need ten thousand, fast."

"You said something about time."

He nodded, sucked smoke, let it out. "Bank examiner's coming in two weeks. The scheduling got changed around. I thought I had another three months, and figured I could raise it somehow...."

Probably the same way as today—by hitting up his soft-hearted old mother.

"If I'm found out," he said, with a desperate shrug, "I'll go to jail. Even if the bank covers it up, to save embarrassment... word will get around. They'll check up on me. Never find a new home at any bank anywhere."

"I'm not getting any younger, son."

He blinked at her again. "What? I know that. What do you...?"

"I've been watching the 700 Club a good deal."

His frown said confusion, not irritation. "Uh, you have? What...Maw, I'm in *trouble*."

"You should tune in, then. Send in your prayer request. Pat Robertson himself will talk to the Lord on your behalf. He's got a pipeline, straight up."

"Are you okay, Maw? Are you...is your *thinking* okay?"

"My thinking's fine. I'm not senile, son, not yet. But I'm coming to terms with my mortality. Thinking about the next stage of life."

Daniel squinted at her. She could almost see him thinking, *The next stage of life for you, Maw, is the cemetery.*

"I've done some bad things in my day, Daniel. Wicked things. Maybe I should make up for it. Maybe donate to the 700 Club to help them spread the Good Word."

"Donate? Well, if you want to. If you...you know, don't overdo."

Another sip of Bud. "I'm thinking I might leave everything to the 700 Club. Thousands and thousands of dollars, son. The whole damn pile. Not a measly little ten grand."

His mouth hung open and his eyes seemed almost as wide.

She said, lightly, "There's another option, though."

Daniel perked up. "Oh?"

"The Precious Moments people."

"What about them?"

"I might have enough to donate to them, too. Spread it around some."

"They're a business, Maw."

She nodded—yes, yes, yes. "A business doing good. Established by preachers. You know, they have that chapel in Carthage. Your brother took me there. Maybe I have enough for those good people to build a Mabel Winifred Comfort wing onto that chapel."

He sat forward. "Maw...I was counting on...you're my *mother*. And I'm your only living child."

"I am. And you are." *A child is right,* she thought.

His smile was a pitiful thing. "Can you *loan* me that money, Maw? Leave the rest to Pat Robertson or Precious Moments or God Himself. But help me keep from having my life and everything I've made of myself slip through my damn fingers? Set up a payment plan. Please?"

She reached across and touched his hand; squeezed it gently. The gesture, not a common one to her, surprised him—almost like it carried an electric shock.

"You can have twenty thousand now," she said, "and all of the rest when I pass."

For a moment he looked as if she'd struck him hard in the belly. Then he relaxed, face softening into relief. "Maw, I knew you'd come through for me. I *knew* you would."

And she had before. This was not the first time he'd come asking for money. She'd always given it to him, because it had been small change—a few hundred for Christmas presents for his wife and kids, a thousand for a family trip. Why not? What was a mother for?

But this time was different. This time he was showing a glimmer of something. This time he'd gotten smart. He had, in his small way, joined the family business.

"Son," she said, "if you insist on being an Honest John all your life, I can't stop you. But when I'm gone, all of this can be yours."

He smiled. "Even the Elvis paintings?"

"Take one with you today, if you like."

"I was just…"

"I know," she said, chewing peanuts. "You think they're tacky. And you're not wrong. Your brother Coleman was a redneck. But so am I, and so are you, under your suits at the bank and your sporty weekend clothes. I never thought I'd live see a Comfort playing…" She shuddered. "…*golf.*"

He shrugged. "It's a business thing, Maw." He sat forward, his smile different now. "Listen, I can't tell you how much I—"

"Can it. The twenty G's is for a favor."

His eyes narrowed. "What kind of favor, Maw?"

"Nolan."

"Who's Nolan?"

She told him. It took a while. She had him get her another Bud from the fridge before she started in.

"This Nolan, for a lot of years, put crews together for institutional jobs," she said. "Banks, mail trucks, armored cars, jewelry stores, the like. He used your brothers Sam and Cole a few times, but finally things kind of went south. Not bloody, just…they didn't work together no more. But a friend of Nolan's got on

Sam's wrong side, and Sam shot him up some. After that, Nolan must've felt justified, ripping Sam off. Him and some punk kid lobbed in smoke grenades and made it look like a fire."

Daniel seemed to be barely following this. "Lobbed in smoke grenades where?"

"At Sam's place in the boonies up in Michigan. See, we Comforts have taken down too many banks to believe in them. Your brothers and your Maw, too…we always keep our money at home. Sam had the bulk of it in a strongbox, and when he thought his house was on fire, he hauled that box of cash the hell out of there."

"And this Nolan was waiting?"

"He was, and that kid accomplice. Your nephew Billy got killed in the fracas, and your brother Sam got shot. Nolan and the kid left him there to bleed out. But he fooled 'em, Sam did, tough ol' bird, and he planned his retribution while he waited for his boy Terry to get out of stir."

"And then…he and Terry went after Nolan?"

"They did. And got themselves killed for their trouble. Shot-gunned to shit and took the blame for a bank job of Nolan's."

Daniel was nodding, eyes narrowed. "I guess I knew that rap. Cole told me when I asked him about it once. It was in the papers, remember?"

"I do. And the world thinks your poor dead brother pulled that bank heist." She crushed an empty Bud can in her hand and tossed it on the table with a clatter. "It wasn't goddamn fucking fair."

"Sam getting the blame?"

"No! Sam not getting the money! Are you paying attention, Daniel?"

"I am, Maw. But what is the point?"

She leaned in. "I have information about Nolan. It's six months old, but it should still be good. About where he lives, and his business…"

"Well, we *know* his business," Daniel said, shrugging. "He's a pro thief."

"No, son. He's retired. Well, not retired—gone straight. He owns a restaurant or a nightclub or some goddamn shit, that he plowed his ill-gotten gains into. Anyway, the money ain't my concern."

That sent her son's eyebrows up. "It isn't?"

"No! We're making money hand over fist, here. When I pass, you will inherit all of my money *and* this business, if you can grow the balls to run it."

He was thinking now. "The fencing operation."

"That's right. Then you can keep that little chippie happy with cars and clothes. Sell that house that got you in trouble. Move in here. Take down the Elvis pictures, and John Wayne, too. Tear the place down and build your dream house, if you like. I don't give two shits."

"Maw…you're wonderful."

"I know it. Now, it's all yours, *if*…"

"If?"

"…if you do me that favor. The Nolan favor."

"What *about* Nolan?"

"You need to corner him, boy, and make him tell you what happened to your brother. Make him confess. Do whatever it takes."

"Maw, he sounds…dangerous…"

"He's that, all right."

"And that will do it? Find out from him what happened to Cole? That's the favor?"

"Oh, hell no. Son, you have to kill the bastard."

"I'm no killer!"

She flipped a dismissive hand at him. "Then you're no son of mine. And the only decision you leave me to make is between Pat Robertson and Precious Moments."

"Maw, you can't ask this of me."

"I *am* asking you, boy. I want that man's head."

"I…have to *kill* him. You want him dead."

"Yes. I want his head."

"Figure of speech."

"Figure it any way you like." She rose. "Wait here."

Maw didn't even use her walker. She was energized. She trundled into Coleman's bedroom and selected just the right one.

On her return, she placed the basket in front of Daniel, who reacted like a startled child, which was what he was, wasn't he? She lifted the lid gingerly, like a Hindu snake charmer checking the contents.

"Use this," she said.

He swallowed thickly. He was close to crying, she knew; but to his credit, he didn't. Maybe he was a Comfort after all.

"And bring it here," she said.

"Yes, Maw."

2.

Business tonight at Nolan's was slow, but business overall was good. This was a Thursday, always the quiet before the weekend storm, and the owner/manager of the nightclub/restaurant had no complaints...other than boredom, perhaps. He preferred it hopping, because that meant time went fast and profits piled up. For a man who seemed so calm and self-composed—enough so that he could make other people nervous—Nolan had a restlessness that required action.

Or anyway activity. At fifty-five he was not unhappy to be free of the twenty years he'd spent running from mob guys and helming high-end robberies, pursuits that had overlapped in sometimes harrowing ways. This set-up was what he had trained for in Chicago, in the early days before he alienated a top wise guy, whose brother he killed, which was a big part of the alienation.

Now Nolan was back to square one, but in a good way. The money he'd accumulated in the heisting years had bought him this nice slice of the American Dream. The place had been an ersatz TGI Fridays when he opened it, all barnwood booths and nostalgic tin signs and old movie posters; but he had remodeled over the winter.

Now Nolan's, despite its mall location, was a classic supper club, high-end dark wood paneling and endless polished bar, black-and-white-checked marble floor, white-linen tables, framed photos of movie stars and recording artists from his era, and in the men's room framed pin-up prints by Vargas and Petty. Fridays and Saturdays, a portable maple dance floor was set up in the side room, where a local combo played and their vocalist, a pretty black girl from Rock Island, sang the Great American Songbook.

Sherry had hated the idea at first, until she saw the crowds stream in, thanks to a great write-up in the *Quad City Times*. Her only complaint about the clientele had been a whispered, "They're so old," but he had told his twenty-three-year-old hostess (and live-in lover), "Not any older than me. Some are even younger."

"Might be a fad," she'd said.

He shrugged. "Then we'll ride it out and do something else."

Sherry, slender, pert-breasted, blue-eyed, Bardot-lipped, her shoulder-brushing light brown hair frosted blonde, had soon traded in her funky Madonna-ish threads for classic cocktail dresses. He even caught her humming songs written long before she was born. Educating the girl was the least he could do, considering what she did for him.

Leaning an elbow against the bar, not taking up one of the stools, Nolan made a distinctive host—rangy with dark, well-barbered widow's-peaked hair, gray at the temples, cheekbones on loan from an Apache, eyes narrow and permanently suspicious. His chevron mustache, carefully trimmed and free of gray, added more than a hint of Western gunfighter.

He wore a milk-chocolate Armani suit with wide shoulders and pleated pants and a dark-chocolate collarless shirt, and black Ferragamo wingtips. As a man tight with a dollar, he did not like to think how much this (and other togs in a recently refurbished wardrobe) had set him back, but Sherry had insisted.

"You invested in making this place classy," she said. "Now it's your turn."

She reminded him it was all deductible and, further, that how he presented himself as the Nolan of Nolan's was crucial.

The kitchen closed at nine, fifteen minutes from now. At her hostess station, in her perfectly coiffed hair and low-cut black lace cocktail dress, Sherry looked like the world's most beautiful female preacher standing at her pulpit. He could tell she was working at keeping that pleasant expression going, fighting boredom, checking her watch every couple of minutes—her hostess duties ended when the kitchen's did.

She glanced at him, made a funny face, and he curled a finger at her. Her eyebrows went up, making the big blue eyes bigger. He used his entire hand now, summoning her like a plane coming in for a landing.

The black lace dress was tight enough to make the trip take longer than might seem possible as she came over and planted herself before him.

"Thirteen minutes to go," she said.

She was standing closer than decorum might advise. Bobby Darin was singing "The Good Life" on the sound system, softly, but you could make out every word.

"The waitresses can handle any strays," Nolan said. "Fred can tally up the registers and lock up."

"What do you have in mind?"

"Looking for a little quality time with my girl. Is that a crime?"

They traded lazy little smiles.

She said, "You must think I'm an easy lay."

"Here's hoping."

They lived on the Illinois side of the Quad Cities, in Moline, up the hill off 16th Street in a trendy housing development, a drive that took half an hour from the mall restaurant, depending on traffic. The two didn't speak on the way, not a word. He had something on his mind and she could obviously sense that, though some of her glances said she wasn't sure whether she was in for a literal kiss or a figurative slap.

He left the car radio tuned to her favorite station—the fare running to Bangles, Madonna, Heart, and Starship—and neither complained nor switched to Easy Listening. He'd never admitted it to her, but really he was fine with what she liked, having grown up when rock 'n' roll got going. Besides, he got enough of Tony Bennett and Peggy Lee and the various Rat Pack boys at work.

It was just that he had a subject he didn't want to broach in the car. If she read that wrong, that was up to her. He'd straighten her out soon enough.

They'd been together, off and on, for about four years. When they started, she'd been on the planet for less than two decades while he had been breathing for a half a century. Even now, the age difference lifted eyebrows, but had been nobody's business until maybe the last year or so. He was getting respectable. He belonged to two country clubs. He was a member of the Chamber of Commerce.

A golfing buddy had said, kidding on the square, "That girl you live with is young enough to be your daughter."

"Right," Nolan said. "But you know what the best part is?"

"No, what?"

"She isn't."

Sherry had been his employee when they met, a kid who'd just graduated junior college working a summer job in the restaurant of the Tropical Motel, which Nolan had run for the Chicago Outfit for a while after he and they made peace. He let others with experience in the hospitality industry handle the heavy lifting on the motel side—nightclubs and restaurants were his strong suit.

He was well aware that waitressing was hard, underrated work, but right off the bat this girl Sherry had a handle on the key elements, from math skills to customer service, from speed to efficiency. Still, her best quality—people skills—proved her greatest weakness. She would chat up customers and get distracted and food would slide from trays and drinks would get spilled. The latter wasn't always accidental.

With her curvy coed's body wrapped up in a short-skirted green uniform, Sherry's pleasantness would unwittingly encourage men to get fresh and, more than once, she had poured hot coffee into the lap of a would-be Romeo. Nolan had almost fired her twice.

That culminated in the head waitress coming to his office at the rear of the restaurant to say she'd just handled a third such infraction on Sherry's part.

"How upset is the patron, Doris?" he asked her.

The forty-something bottle blonde, with heavy makeup and a world of experience, said, "He was screaming. Maybe a lot of that was the coffee in his crotch. I said there'd be no charge for his meal and he stormed back to his room to clean himself up."

"Ah. A guest with the motel."

"Yes. His friends are still here. They just put their orders in. His included. I imagine he'll be back for his free meal."

Nolan nodded. "Send the girl back here."

She did.

Soon he was saying to the crying waitress, "This is the third goddamn lap you've spilled hot coffee into. How is that even possible?"

She had tearfully explained: "They were all dirty old men."

"No shortage of those. Sometimes you have to cut these creeps some slack."

"This one said I had a nice ass."

The customer is always right, Nolan thought, but said, "Sometimes you have to look the other way. Some of our guests are rough around the edges."

They had patrons from Chicago who made the trip to the Tropical near DeKalb to get away, have a swim, play a little golf, boink their girlfriends or even sometimes their wives, and also to talk business in private. The FBI wasn't wise to the Tropical, so the rooms weren't watched or wired. Nolan made sure of that.

"How out of line," Nolan asked her, "did this guest get?"

"I told you," she said, chin quivering. "He said I had a nice ass." She swallowed. "And he had his hand on it at the time."

"Just patted it or…?"

"Grabbed it. I asked him to let go and he didn't and I pulled away and…poured his coffee."

That sounded like self-defense.

"Point out the table," Nolan said, rising, "where his friends are sitting."

She followed him to the office door and hid behind him, peeking around.

"There he is," she whispered. "Just sitting down."

Returning from his room with a change of wardrobe below the belt. Not that guys like that ever changed below the belt.

Nolan knew him from an earlier visit to the Tropical—a low-level Outfit guy named Joe Something, joining three other bent-nose boys at a center table. They were in pastel shirts and plaid shorts and hairy legs and black socks.

"Okay," he said. "Get back out on the floor. You're needed."

"Yes, sir."

Nolan released her into the wild, waited a minute or so, then headed over to the four men at their table. The Tropical's restaurant was nothing fancy, just a step up from a truck-stop diner, with only some half-ass plastic parrot art and fake Hawaiian-type flowers and plants to spice up the walls. Not his dream job, but at least he was back in solid with the Outfit.

"Gentlemen," Nolan said, leaning in, smiling, but no one smiled back; these were the kind of expressions you saw at the track when a horse hadn't come in. "Joe, there's a call for you in my office."

Nolan and Joe chatted amiably as they walked to the rear of the dining area, and inside the office, with the door closed, Nolan slipped an arm around Joe, who looked a little like a sinister version of that fat cop on *Car 54 Where Are You?*.

Joe, noting the phone on its hook, looked confused. "What call?"

"No call. I just want a word. I have no desire to embarrass you in public."

"Why would you embarrass me in public?"

"Because you embarrassed a staff member of mine. In public."

A thick upper lip peeled back over cigarette-stained teeth. "You *do* know who I work for?"

"I know exactly who you work for."

"That's good," Joe said gruffly.

"Which is why I wanted a private word. We're happy here at the Tropical to provide a place where my Chicago friends can get away for a day or two. To relax. Eat well. Catch some sun and swim. Or even do business in privacy."

He shrugged big shoulders. "Place is nothin' fancy, but it's okay."

"Right. Well, thing is—we're also a family place. People from nearby towns come here. Sycamore, DeKalb, Geneva. So you could do me a favor."

"Name it."

"Tell the boys to keep their hands off the waitresses. These are not hookers, they're college girls and locals."

Joe slipped out from under Nolan's arm and his face got red

as he shook a fist at his host. "Who the fuck do you think you are, talkin' to me like that?"

"I think I'm the guy," Nolan said cheerfully, "who shot Big Charlie's brother and got away with it."

Then he put his hand in Joe's face and pushed him, startling him. The fat boy staggered back, blinking, and then Nolan started slapping him. Three slaps that rang in the room.

Astonished, Joe stood there, panting.

"Questions?" Nolan asked.

Joe shook his head.

"I'll get the check for your entire party. Rooms, too. Enjoy your stay."

Nolan opened the office door for the guy and gestured for him to go out, which he did, huffing and puffing as he went.

Sherry, serving some customers on the floor and managing not to empty her tray on any of them, watched with big blue eyes as Nolan wandered into the well-populated restaurant with its plastic flora and fauna and stood with folded arms as the fat patron and his three thuggish friends got up, all four glaring back at Nolan, but saying nothing as they hauled ass out.

Sherry smiled at him.

Nolan nodded at her.

Back in his office, Nolan made a call to his contact with the Outfit, a lawyer named Felix who had a single, albeit important, client. He reported the incident.

"I'll take care of it," Felix said. "We can't have our people shitting where they eat."

"You can't have them shitting where my customers eat. You want me out of here, say the word."

"No. You were within bounds."

"I don't have to kill anybody?"

"No. Not unless they do something foolish before I can get

the word out, then…by all means, do whatever. They're low-level. Not Family."

"Got it. Thanks."

Goodbyes were said, phones hung up.

Toward the end of the afternoon, a knock came on Nolan's door. He opened his right-hand desk drawer, where a .38 long-barreled revolver kept itself available, and reached his hand in, settling it around the gun's grip, saying, "Yeah."

Sherry, looking remarkably fresh for end of shift, asked from the doorway. "May I come in, Mr. Logan?"

That was the name he'd been using lately.

"Please." He took his hand off the weapon.

She shut the door and came over to the desk, where no chair was provided since Nolan preferred not to talk to people that long.

"I wanted to thank you," she said, standing there, "for throwing those men out."

"You're welcome."

"That man who put his hand on my bottom…" Suddenly she couldn't bring herself to say "ass." He thought that was cute. "…his cheeks were red. And I don't think it was because he was mad or embarrassed. There were little tiny…blood droplets."

"Slap somebody hard enough, that can happen."

She smiled; she clasped her hands before her, like a kid about to dig into Christmas. "You stuck up for me. I spill coffee in a customer's lap, and you stick up for me."

She hustled around and spilled herself into his lap.

Of course, he'd had to remove her from the wait staff, but the Tropical's restaurant could use a hostess evenings, when the menu got smaller and pricier, and with her people skills, she was perfect. Also, he gave her a big raise. Of course, she gave him plenty of big raises over the rest of a glorious summer.

The girl's plan had been to go back to college in the fall, but her father had a stroke and died, and things got derailed. Her mother's health hadn't been good, either—the woman passed a year ago. When Nolan acquired the restaurant at Brady Eighty Mall in Davenport, he'd called Sherry, who'd filled him in on all that, and told her he had a position to offer her.

"Would that be," she said, "the Missionary Position?"

They had talked to each that way all the time that summer at the Tropical, and the remark erased the months since they'd last cohabited.

"No," Nolan said, "it's a hostess position. The other would be optional."

"A perk?"

"Yes. Many such perks will be on offer."

"Cool. Where and when do you want me?"

That question sparked more nonsense, but eventually he filled her in on addresses and other details.

The driveway was just to the right as Nolan pulled into his street. The sprawling Fifties-modern one-story was set against a wooded area, the yard in back dipping down to expose the finished basement. Deer would sometimes stroll right up to the glass doors and just look in like you were a zoo animal. Nolan loved that, though he didn't know why—the wildness in him, his throwback nature to another time, was something he never noticed.

He had never owned a house before. Often he'd lived in digs provided by his mobbed-up bosses, and back in thieving days he had been in this apartment and that one. Some lodgings had been nice enough—a number had been condos—but having his own roof over his head made him feel he had finally arrived.

And now it was time to make another change, though not of domicile.

After he pulled his silver Trans Am into the garage, they went inside, separately. That was not unusual—for the same reasons that he kept his back to walls in a bar or restaurant, Nolan invariably entered his house by the rear entrance. It required walking all around the house to access the door of that finished basement. Still he did it.

For a while he'd convinced Sherry to do that, too, but finally she wouldn't put up with it. Getting her shoes muddy walking around the house to get back there put an end to it. When they were already in the garage, with the connecting door right there—why not just go in? Even after the place had been invaded that time by those gay hitmen, she hadn't learned the lesson. Even after Cole Fucking Comfort kidnapped her six months ago, she hadn't learned.

Sometimes you couldn't tell a woman anything.

She was in the kitchen leaning against the counter, still in her black lace cocktail dress, when he caught up with her.

She asked, "You want coffee?"

"No."

"Decaf?"

"No."

"Sandwich? Leftover pasta?"

They often had a bite to eat before bed. Working restaurant hours, going in at four (opening at five), they started their day with breakfast and had a very early supper before work, usually grabbing fast food or Denny's. Sometimes the chef fixed them up at Nolan's.

"No food," he said. "I'm fine. Thanks."

"Talkative all of a sudden."

"I do want to talk."

She frowned at him. "Is this an argument? Are we mad about something? Because I didn't notice."

"No. Just…we need to talk."

"The four worst words in the English language, when you string them together." She gestured to the table. "Why don't I fix coffee for us? And we'll get into whatever it is."

"No. We'll talk in bed. I'm going to shower."

"Okay," she said, her expression puzzled now.

He showered. Thoughts were going quickly, his head filled with words at odds with how little he'd shared with her so far. He soaped himself thoroughly, rinsed in water as hot as he could take it, then toweled off, using the hair drier as if he was stalling. Maybe he was. He splashed on Old Spice, a habit he'd never broken, and looked at his naked self in the mirror.

So many scars angling through the body hair. Bullet wounds. Knife wounds. He shook his head. Sherry had all that untouched perfect pink flesh going for her with only an appendectomy scar to prove she'd been on the planet fifteen minutes. He, on the other hand, looked fifty-five. No. Fifty-five miles of bad road.

He didn't bother with his robe, stepping out into the adjacent master bedroom, bare-ass.

Sherry, in her sheer panties (no bra—not necessary), was stretched out on her side of the bed, nightstand lamp on, as she read a hardcover book, *Misery* by Stephen King. She was amused. By him, not King.

"Well," she said, with half a smile. "Does your mother let you go out in public like that?"

"I didn't ask permission," he said with the other half of the smile.

She slipped off the bed and out of the panties, which she pitched carelessly somewhere, and moved quickly into the bathroom, where the sound of the shower's needles soon followed.

He lay on his back on the bed, where she'd warmed it, and

just thinking about her naked in there, all pearled with water, rubbing herself with soap, got him hard. He was that way when she emerged bundled into her green plush oversize robe, toweling off her hair.

"I am not so brazen as you, Mr. Nolan," she said. Then she stopped toweling and noticed him standing at attention lying down and said, "What have you got there for me?"

"Hope it speaks for itself."

"So do I."

She tossed the towel. Opened her robe. The long sleek legs, the trimmed pubic thatch, that impossibly narrow waist, the B-cup breasts with erect nipples in their pink circles, all worked together to make his dick dance. He got to his feet. She came over, her hair damp in gypsy tendrils, dropped the robe into a puddle that she knelt on, and engulfed him in the caress of her full-lipped mouth.

He almost lost the war, but retreated in time, then got down there on the floor and buried his head between her legs and licked and nuzzled and made her moan and squirm. They took turns riding each other, on the puddled robe, then he bent her over the edge of the bed and did what every heterosexual man who had ever caught a glimpse of that ass wanted to do.

They staggered together into the bathroom, and she was looking at him in the big mirror when he said, "Will you marry me?"

3.

Jon, too, was back at square one.

Nolan's twenty-five year-old former accomplice in crime—the top down on his decade-old red Mustang convertible—was heading west on Tropicana Avenue to a strip-mall comic book shop, the third he'd checked out today.

When he'd first come to Vegas, he'd checked out all such shops, as any relocating diehard comic book fan would, to see which he wanted to frequent. This was the third of the three he'd decided not to do business with. But he had something more on his mind on these visits than where to buy his weekly stack of comics.

Jon was small but muscular, with short curly blond hair and blue eyes and a baby face. He wore a vintage Wonder Warthog t-shirt, blue jeans and sandals. He didn't mind the summer heat of Vegas at all, which was so much drier without the Midwestern humidity he was used to. Just the same, he was frowning.

In thought.

A lot had happened in the five years since his late uncle had put him together with Nolan for what at the time was meant to be Jon's first job and Nolan's last. Robbing the bank in Port City, Iowa—with the inside help of a girl he knew who worked there—had been Jon's own bright idea. The job came off, but a lot of people got killed along the way, which was indirectly on him.

No civilians died, as Nolan had put it, and that was the important thing. Still, any death attached to committing a crime was felony murder for all participants, and carried the highest of risks.

Had Jon been raised differently, the guilt of all that might have been enough to put him on another path. Certainly armed robbery wasn't the profession he had hoped to grow up to pursue.

And you might think the comic books and strips he'd read in his formative years and beyond, with heroes like Superman, Batman and Dick Tracy, would have taught him about truth, justice and the American way, and crime not paying, although the Dark Knight's message (especially post-Adam West) was more one of vengeance, when you got right down to it.

But when an older Jon got around to collecting pricier vintage funny books, his passion became the 1950s horror comics so reviled by polite society, tales of terror that had little to do with heroes, though quite a bit with villains. These grisly stories often suggested life was a horrific shithole indeed. Jon could relate.

His mother, who sang and played piano in restaurants, bars and lounges, always thinking a big break was over the blue horizon, shuttled him for years from one relative to another; his father had been an unidentified flying object that took flight before Jon was born. Bouncing around through his childhood with uncles and aunts wound up with him never lighting anywhere long enough to make friends who weren't four-color figments.

And none of the men his mother shacked up with lasted long enough for Jon to get more out of them than the occasional beating. Only rarely had she worked a gig that kept her in one place long enough for Jon to join her. When she got hit by a car, it was thought she might have stepped in front of it on purpose. When he learned of it, Jon had been halfway across the country in high school (he attended seven of those, but not her funeral).

The last relative he landed with had been his uncle Ed in Iowa City. The old antiques dealer had provided a kindred spirit for the boy, sharing with him a love for all things nostalgic; they grew so close that Jon even stayed on after turning eighteen, going to the University of Iowa for three semesters, which his uncle paid for.

His uncle's last name, as far as the authorities knew, was Planner, which was sort of an inside joke. The antique shop the old boy ran was mostly a front, a cover for the outlining of institutional robberies and the occasional private residence. While his uncle never participated in a robbery on site, he was an expert at casing targets and working up plans for pulling off scores, right down to floor plans, diagrams, maps and even blueprints.

Looking back on it, Jon could see how a basically decent kid like himself could accept that left-handed way of living as an acceptable one. Planner was a sweet old guy, not a mean bone in his body, and had explained often to his nephew that he only planned robberies whose ultimate victim was either an insurance company or the wealthy. As a child of the counterculture of the late '60s and early '70s, Jon did not view the Establishment with much sympathy.

And then there was Nolan.

Nolan, who might have been Lee Van Cleef crawled down off the screen out of a Sergio Leone western, had been a frequent Planner collaborator. He ran crews, tight ships where collateral damage was not allowed—Jon never quite knew whether that constraint mattered to Nolan because of the consequences homicide might bring or out of an innate sense of decency.

But Nolan was not a mean guy, unless crossed, and Jon didn't know of anyone Nolan ever killed who wasn't another bad guy who earned the honor, or a sociopath like either Sam or Cole Comfort, nightmare modern-day hillbillies who would rather murder than not.

Jon and Nolan got along well, almost from the start, despite the decades and experiences that separated them. They became more than colleagues. They were friends. The younger man was not self-aware enough to realize Nolan was the father figure that Jon's mother had denied him, and would have laughed that idea off anyway, if nervously.

What Jon did know, and liked, was that Nolan had gone straight. That while they had pulled a few more jobs together, when something out of the older man's past popped up requiring action (and presenting the possibility of pulling in some cash), both Nolan and Jon had stepped away from lives of crime.

Now Nolan was running a restaurant/nightclub in the Quad Cities, where Jon had briefly joined him when Cole Comfort rose from his swamp to blackmail them into robbing that mall. But now Comfort was dead and the mall was doing just fine, and so was Nolan.

Jon had carved out some success with *Space Pirates*, an independent comic book that was a cultish success, though that had hit a snag lately when the small-time publisher of *Pirates* and a few other quirky books went belly-up. No other publisher had stepped up to fill the void, and Jon was considering self-publishing. But of course that required capital.

He had also kept himself solvent, more or less, with his sideline as a musician. At the last high school he'd attended, he'd played keyboards in a rock band that played homecoming dances and proms; and in the two years he spent as an undergrad at the U of Iowa, his combo played frats and bars.

That had led to another, more professional band, fronted by Toni, a girlfriend of his. The Nodes had some college radio success with an album, which was mostly songs Jon wrote. But that hadn't led to anything more, and Toni caught a break and was singing back-up now for Prince, leaving Jon high and dry.

With Toni's apartment rented out from under him, Jon had no alternative but to crash at Nolan's house in Moline, where he got caught up in the Comfort mall mess. But in the aftermath, Jon knew he was a third wheel getting in Nolan and his girl Sherry's way. So he'd asked Nolan for help.

They'd chatted in the finished basement of Nolan's house, shooting pool. Jon was good enough to win money playing at the rear of the Airliner bar in Iowa City, but Nolan was a wizard. He would run the balls before you even got a turn. Jon didn't care. He just wanted to talk.

"I was wondering," Jon said.

"Five in the corner pocket….What are you wondering?"

"I could put a combo together for Nolan's."

"Not against it. Nine in the left side pocket."

"*Space Pirates* is doing okay, but it's not a living, not yet, anyway. How much do you think you could afford for a band? What kind of music? How many nights?"

"Charity or real world?"

"Real world."

"Seven in the corner pocket….Not sure what music would work. I'm thinking of remodeling and that would mean jazz or standards. That isn't your thing."

"You're right, it's not. Anybody else in the Cities you can think of that maybe could work?"

"No. Eightball in the side pocket….Another round?"

Jon took the break, sunk two solid colors, then missed the next shot.

Nolan said, "Three in the side pocket….How do you feel about Vegas?"

"This time of year…" It was cold and icy outside, the world

through the glass doors a Winter Wonderland best viewed from inside. "…it sounds pretty damn good."

"I know a guy. Five in the corner pocket."

"You know a guy?"

Nolan, chalking up, nodded. "Harry Bellows. He's a loud-mouth, which makes it easy to remember his name. I knew him on Rush Street, years ago, and we got friendly again, after I got off the Family shit list."

"He's in Vegas?"

Nolan nodded again, then leaned in for his shot. "Seven in the corner pocket.…He's a casino exec at the French Quarter."

"I thought you said this was Vegas."

"It is Vegas. Everything in Vegas is named after somewhere else. French Quarter is way out, beyond the Strip. Kind of a world unto itself. Attracts a lot of your Baby Boomer crowd. They book Oldies Acts. They might have a house band you could play in. Nine in the corner pocket."

Jon's band had been New Wave, doing stuff that derived from Sixties music. He could handle a gig like that. "That would be great."

"I'll make a phone call.…Eightball in the side pocket.… Another round?"

So for the last almost six months, Jon had been playing in the Creole Showroom at the French Quarter, in the house band, two guitars, drums, bass guitar and keyboards. He'd backed up some incredible acts from the past—Del Shannon, Chuck Berry, Bobby Rydell, Gene Pitney, he could hardly keep track. Frankie Avalon and Fabian were wrapping up an engagement now, but Jon had next week off, because the Everly Brothers were coming in with their own all-star back-up band.

He pulled the Mustang into the parking lot of a shabby-looking strip mall. No tumbleweed was blowing through the cramped parking lot, but he wouldn't have been surprised if it had been. Neon Comics was at the dead end of a lineup of uninspiring shops—laundromat, video rental, shoes, dry cleaning, sub sandwiches. Directly across the way was another such strip mall, anchored by a Tower Records in the middle. That encouraged Jon—that place *always* did good business. Might mean overflow, if you had something to offer....

Neon Comics had a painted sign above the front window, which to Jon said it all. He strolled into the comic book shop—the fat bearded guy eating a Big Mac behind the counter did not look up from his current issue of *X-Men* to greet his customer—and had a look around. This was Wednesday afternoon, the day the new comic books came out, but it was deader than disco. New issues were not displayed anywhere. No posters were on the walls; no original artwork; no toys or action figures or models. Plastic-bagged Golden and Silver Age comics clipped in drooping double rows hung on the facing side walls. Bagged comics in boxes were on tables vertically arranged in the narrow store, whose lighting was courtesy of buzzing blue-tinged florescent tubes.

Jon asked the fat bearded guy behind the counter if he was the owner.

He did not look up from his comic. "No."

Jon handed him a slip of paper with his phone number and address. "Can you give that to the owner?"

Still no eye contact. "Okay."

Jon left smiling. He could do a better job with a comic book shop in his fucking sleep. They *couldn't* be doing any business, and he saw no indication that this was a front for selling grass or anything, which might have explained things. But they had a good inventory of older comics, and of more current stuff, too. Landing that space, with its corner location, and trumpeting new management, would be helpful; but the inventory was the key.

From the strip mall to his apartment in Paradise, Nevada, an unincorporated suburb and home to the casino-flung Strip, took Jon just twenty minutes. The Havenwood Apartments was a cluster of two-story gray clapboard buildings with exterior metal staircases; but the courtyard boasted a pool, and his one-bedroom apartment had carpet, a full electric kitchen and a working air conditioner. Also, scorpions, but at three-fifty a month, he couldn't expect any better in this town.

His drafting table dominated one side of the living room, adjacent to the kitchenette. The rest was given over to his Sony 21-inch TV on a stand, with VHS recorder/player beneath. A thriftshop bookcase nearby held hardcover collections of his favorite comics (mostly newspaper strips) with a shelf of VHS pre-records and another shelf with a small boombox for playing the CDs also stored there. Down toward the far windows, a couch, also secondhand, faced the TV. More Goodwill Store furniture could be found in his bedroom. Both the living room and bedroom walls were plastered with posters—Mr. Spock, the Man With No Name, *Batman* #1, *Superman* #1, *Amazing Fantasy* #15 (Spiderman's debut), *Avengers* #1, and so on.

He was well aware that he was still living like a college student, but if he could make a comic book shop happen, everything would come together.

That was when he remembered.

Remembered that opening and running his own comic book shop had been the dream he'd hoped to finance with the bank robbery that had started everything. That had led to lives being lost and all the mayhem that followed.

Full circle.

He chuckled to himself, shook his head, and sat at his

drafting board and worked at inking a page of *Space Pirates*. As he did, he thought about what he might say to Nolan. He didn't want to ask for a loan. He didn't want to ask his friend to invest. Both made him uncomfortable, and anyway he knew Nolan to be something of a tightwad. The idea of putting his friend on the spot, much less having to hear the man turn him down, wasn't at all attractive.

The phone rang.

He put down his pen, wiped some ink from his hands with a rag, and headed over to the couch and sat, grabbing the phone off the hook from its perch on a (yes) thriftshop end table.

"Jon speaking."

"Jon, Randy Davis. With Neon Comics."

"Yeah, Randy. I hoped to see you today. I should have called before dropping by."

"Are you the *Space Pirates* guy?"

"Guilty."

"Listen, it's a great book. We sold five copies of the last issue."

Wow. Talk about endorsements.

"But, uh," the comic shop owner was saying, "I don't think doing a signing with us would be worth your time. We got our regulars, who come in for the books they have us pull for 'em, but other than that, we don't get much foot traffic."

"Randy, I didn't stop by about setting up a signing."

"No?"

"No, I wondered if you might be interested in selling."

"Selling what?"

"Neon Comics. Your shop."

"Oh! Oh. Might be. Might be. I've been thinking about getting into baseball cards, though. You know, expanding."

"With another location?"

"No, just…bringing the cards in to kind of supplement the comics."

This was bullshit. They didn't begin to have room for that.

The two talked for a while. Jon got the picture—Randy would sell the "good will" and the inventory, and sign over the lease for the space, which was good for another three years at $400 a month.

"Ten grand," Jon said.

"I'm thinking twenty."

"I'd be committing to another $15,000 by taking on the lease and that doesn't include taxes. Ten."

Randy argued a while, but finally he took the deal.

"Give me a month," Jon said, "to get the payment together."

"Okay. I'll work on the paperwork. You show me your lawyer, I'll show you mine."

After hanging up, Jon sat there thinking about how to approach Nolan. With remodeling that shop a must, he would need thirty grand to make this fly. How could he talk Nolan into what he had in mind?

One last job?

The phone rang.

"Jon," Jon said into the receiver.

"Nolan."

"Oh. Nolan. Hello."

Jon could have counted the calls Nolan had made to him over the years on his fingers, and have plenty of fingers left.

"You won't believe this," Jon said, "but I was just thinking about calling you. Something I want to talk about."

"Well, we'll have a chance, if you're around next week. In Vegas, I mean."

"I will be, yeah. I even have some time off. Why…?"

"Sherry and I are flying out Wednesday."

This was Saturday. A midweek trip made sense—weekend flights were more expensive, and Nolan being Nolan....

"Well," Jon said, "we'll have to get together!"

This was a nice break—it would give him a chance to talk face to face, eyeball to eyeball.

"Count on it," Nolan said.

Jon said, "You want tickets to the Everly Brothers? I can make that happen. My treat. I think I can help get you a nice room at the French Quarter."

"Thanks, the concert tickets would be fine, but Harry Bellows lined up a penthouse suite there for us."

"You must be doing well at that joint of yours, to splurge like that."

"Well, you don't get married every day."

"What?"

"I don't repeat myself on long distance."

"Nolan, that's great."

And it was. Any man would be lucky to land a beautiful smart woman like Sherry. Even if Nolan *was* old enough to be her father....

"That's why I'm calling," Nolan said. "I'm going to need a best man."

Jon found himself surprisingly touched. "I'd be honored."

"Good. That's taken care of. What was it you wanted to talk about?"

"It'll wait."

4.

As she sat in her robe at the kitchen table the morning after she said yes to his proposal of marriage, Sherry listened while Nolan arranged by phone what was obviously the best deal on a ceremony he could wangle at the Little Church of the West in Las Vegas.

"Photos and bouquet yes," he told the wall-mounted phone. He was in his boxer shorts and, with all his scarring, looked like an aging fighter who'd had a rough career. "How much without the photos?"

She frowned at him.

"Can you do better?" he asked the phone. The reply must have been positive, because Nolan told it, "Okay. That will work. No. Not the Elvis package....I don't care if Elvis married Ann-Margret at your chapel in *Viva Las Vegas*. I never saw an Elvis movie in my life....Okay. Thanks."

After he hung up and joined her over coffee at the table, she said teasingly, "We could be married by Elvis and you said no? Where's your sense of fun?"

"I never had one." He sipped coffee. "You'll like the place. It's the oldest wedding chapel in Vegas. It's intimate. And it's not like we're having guests."

He sent her to Von Maur at the rival mall, North Park, to pick out a new dress with no budgetary restriction. Maybe the S.O.B. really did love her. She wasn't hypocritical enough to wear white, and she had no interest in a train or veil; she picked out a pink lacy thing that stopped above her knees.

Later, as the newly engaged couple drove to their restaurant/club for what would certainly be a busy Friday night, she described the dress to him. She was getting too detailed for his bent and he suggested she just try it on for him later.

"No."

"No?"

"I don't want you to see it before the wedding."

"The *wedding*? You, me, Jon and a Vegas preacher?"

"You do make it sound dreamy. No. I'm just that much of a traditionalist. That superstitious, too. You'll see it when I come down the aisle. I'll be alone, of course. I *could* have been escorted by Elvis...."

"Elvis is dead. It was in all the papers. Are you okay with this? Vegas?"

"I love it."

And she did.

"This five-hundred-dollar pink thing," he said.

"Yeah?"

"Sounds nice."

"Glad you approve."

"Maybe you could wear it as a hostess dress when we get back."

That rated a dirty look. No further discussion of the dress followed.

But throughout the evening at Nolan's, whenever there was a lull, he'd ask her again, "You're okay with Vegas?"

Which was surprisingly thoughtful for this battle-scarred hunk. She did have two sisters, after all, who lived in the Midwest, and he probably figured she might rather get married with them in attendance. At one point he suggested he could fly her sisters into Vegas, too. Pretty good offer coming from a guy so tight with a buck.

"My sisters with me on my honeymoon," she said, with a smirk. "What a dream come true that would be. Shall we ask them to bring their husbands and kids?"

So Vegas it was, just the two of them. They would stay three nights and then get back to their lives. This had nothing to do with cheapness on her prospective husband's part. He'd already promised they would take a real honeymoon trip to Europe, since Sherry had never been. He hadn't been there since just after the war, he said, when he'd been stationed in Germany.

He'd once told her how he'd operated a black-market operation in Berlin, which she figured was likely what had put his entire life on its tenuous track. But that was his business, and she'd never pushed it.

Wednesday morning, they took a direct flight from Moline to Vegas and by early afternoon they were taking care of formalities at the Marriage License Bureau in the Justice Center downtown. She could tell Nolan didn't love being inside a building with a name like that, but the process was quick and painless.

Next stop was the French Quarter Casino and Resort, way out the Strip and half a mile down West Tropicana Ave, a pair of wide buildings in a V looking oddly alone in scrubby emptiness, with a few palm trees for trimming.

"Looks like everything around it got bombed out," he said, "and it's the only thing still standing."

Was he thinking about post-war Germany again? she wondered.

The casually dressed couple left their rental Audi in the vast parking lot, which was perhaps a third filled, and approached the gaudily colorful New Orleans-themed hotel. Sherry leaned her head back and filled her eyes with the kitschy spectacle of the French Quarter's white-trimmed-pink baroque exterior—

like Europe, Vegas was a place she'd never been—but Nolan, pulling their wheeled suitcase, just shrugged in an I've-seen-worse way.

When he slipped his free hand into hers as they headed in, she squeezed in surprised appreciation—it was a rare gesture on his part. They were close, no question, but this was a man who still lived largely inside himself. He was good with acquaintances, like his Chamber of Commerce golfing buddies, but only his young former accomplice Jon had ever seemed to her a real friend of his. She had a hunch Jon's presence was why they were here, not just in Vegas but at the French Quarter itself, since the young musician/cartoonist worked at the place.

Inside, they found themselves not in a lobby or a reception area, but a sudden overwhelming expanse of casino, sprawling, light-flashing, smoky, ding-ding-dinging, with facing wrought-iron-railed balconies and a giant two-faced card-deck joker's head with tiny torso hanging from the high ceiling to laugh silently at the fools throwing away their money. On their own elevated stage a trio of cartoonish musical-instrument-wielding alligators oversaw the slots and video poker, as if the predatory machines needed reinforcement. A reception desk fronted by a big carved purple-and-black domino mask was off to the left and they headed there.

Check-in went fast and within ten minutes they were in their suite. They only had the one bag and no bellboy had been provided, nor had Nolan requested one. The accommodations were devoid of the Mardi Gras theme—just grays and blues with touches of red, the furnishings modern. "That's a relief," Nolan said, stowing their suitcase on a luggage rack.

"What is?"

"None of that Bourbon Street bull."

She agreed—she was happy to leave the New Orleans flavor

downstairs—if a little disappointed he hadn't sprung for the honeymoon suite.

Her husband-to-be was having a look around their digs—common practice for him. Whenever they traveled, he would always get a handle on his surroundings. She was aware he'd lived through a decade and a half of having mobsters looking for him, not to mention demented hicks, so such precautions were built-in now.

"Lot of these Vegas hotels," he said, "are short on the amenities. They want you gambling—don't want anything that might keep you in your room." He gestured. "But this is okay."

She saw what he meant—25-inch TV, small fridge, coffee maker, and of course king-size bed.

He had the closet door open. "Combination safe in here. The only thing in this joint you can put your money in and maybe get it back out."

She was unpacking, putting things away in the dresser.

"Not the honeymoon suite," he said, "but it'll do."

"Oh," she said, maybe too casually, "I thought you booked the honeymoon suite."

He came over behind her and put his arms around her waist and gave her a little squeeze. "I tried. It was booked. It had a hot tub, too."

"Damn it all," she said lightly.

"Maybe next marriage."

She smiled at him over her shoulder and they shared a peck of a kiss. That kind of thing only happened with this lug behind closed doors—she was well aware he hated public displays.

By late afternoon they were trailing out of the hotel again, an odd couple with Nolan in the blue-gray Hugo Boss suit and dark blue tie she'd picked out as part of his wardrobe make-over, and herself in a halter top and torn jeans and garment bag over her shoulder. Anywhere else they would have gotten looks; here, nothing.

The drive to the Hacienda Hotel and Casino took less than ten minutes. The quaint redwood chapel, its steeple to the left of the compact A-framed structure, sat at the casino property's southeast edge, a bizarrely rustic apparition in an oasis of green, tall trees framing it, smaller ones hugging it. It was like a piece of rural Mid-America had fallen from the sky and landed perfectly, not even bothering to kill a wicked witch.

Parking for the church edged up to the wide thoroughfare, and he pulled in, shut off the car, and they sat and stared at each other.

Then she nodded, and he nodded, and they got out, Sherry gathering her purse and the garment bag. They might have been Bonnie and Clyde outside a gas station in 1932, preparing to go in and knock it over. The late afternoon was just turning to a blue-tinged dusk, mountains blue-brown at the horizon, the towers of the Strip not far from here and starting to glow with their neon invitation to the night.

They walked across the well-tended grass past a waist-high rough-wood sign that announced

Little Church of the West
WEDDING CHAPEL.

She spotted, near the double doors to the sanctuary, a short young man in a black tux, western bow tie, and ruffled shirt and took him to be, at first, a greeter from the facility.

But as they drew closer, she saw that it was Jon, with his hair shorter.

The younger man took a few steps forward, closing the distance between them, and a little smile came. Nolan approached without a smile, but with an expression that Sherry knew reflected something vaguely positive. Neither man extended a hand. That ritual wasn't necessary. Neither did they hug. She figured Jon might have been capable of that, but not with Nolan, who under no circumstances would be.

"You look," Nolan said, "like a fucking riverboat gambler."

"Thank you. I always liked Jack Kelly."

She didn't understand that reference at all, but she smiled and nodded at Jon, who did the same to her. That was the extent of their greeting—when the young man had lived at Nolan's place, an initial resentment between them grew into an uncomfortable sexual tension that she felt had sparked Jon's quickly making tracks after everyone had survived the Cole Comfort fiasco. Except Cole Comfort, of course.

Nolan said, "You didn't have to rent a goddamn tux for the occasion."

"I didn't rent it," Jon said.

"*You* own a tux?"

"Hell no. I don't even own a *suit*. This is stage wardrobe from the French Quarter. This is what we wear when we have a corny act to back up, like Johnny Mathis or Frankie Laine."

Nolan winced. Actually winced. "Your taste is in your ass, kid."

"Much as I'm enjoying this warm reunion," Sherry said to Jon, "d'you know if there's a place where I can change?"

"Just the ladies' room," Jon said, opening one of the double doors.

She went inside and got her first look at the open-beamed interior of the chapel—varnished redwood, wood pews too, candles, and stained-glassed windows, with lighting from the ceiling courtesy of a quartet of Victorian lamps. This was not Vegas glitz but a journey into the pioneer days when men like hers were the rule not the exception.

She paused to take in photos of celebrity couples on the

back wall—Betty Grable and Harry James, Zsa Zsa Gabor and George Sanders, Judy Garland and somebody, Mickey Rooney and somebody. Her warm and fuzzy glow was cut just a shade by a sign saying NO CHECKS CASHED next to bridegroom David Cassidy of *The Partridge Family*. Then, despite cramped one-stall quarters, she got into her pink dress and freshened her makeup. Her hair was fine—she'd sprayed it in place back at the French Quarter.

When Sherry emerged, a middle-aged woman was waiting, in cat's-eye glasses, a pink polyester dress, yellow permed hair and makeup as garish as Vegas itself, a bouquet of daisies at the ready.

"You're the bride," the woman said.

"I am."

"I'm Janine Totter, manager here at the chapel. You're in for a lovely experience—my Lloyd and I were married here in 1952 and fell in love with the place....I'm going to guess you don't want your beloved to get a glimpse of you just yet."

"Yes."

"Step into my office."

The maple-paneled office was small and nearly as cramped as the ladies' room. A little portable TV was perched on a desk with not much paperwork, an old *Bewitched* rerun playing, sound barely audible.

"Now," Mrs. Totter said, "we have a wonderful minister today. Reverend Love is a Baptist but here at the Little Church we're non-denominational. God is strictly optional."

"Yes, let's leave Him out of it."

"I'll let that be known," she said cheerily, and handed her the bouquet, adding, "Make yourself at home, dear," then slipped out.

So Sherry stood with bouquet in hand and watched *Bewitched* for a while, thinking it might be a blessing that neither of their mothers were around to turn into Agnes Moorehead.

When a knock came on the door in about ten minutes, a boyishly handsome, fleshy-faced dark-blond man of about fifty, in a sharp tuxedo, was standing there smiling.

"I'm Phil," he said, in resonant tenor. "I have the privilege of walking you down the aisle, if you'll allow it."

"Certainly," she said, somewhat surprised at the chapel providing this service. Had the groom paid extra?

From the rear of the chapel, on the arm of her friendly escort, she saw Nolan and Jon, half-turned to watch her make her way down the modest aisle between the empty pews. She wondered if the forest smell was the redwood itself or room freshener. The minister was positioned as expected, a big man with Brylcreemed hair, a rust-colored suit, and a brown shirt with clerical collar. At left, another middle-aged man who somewhat resembled her escort, but darker-haired, also wore a tux. He was playing the Bridal March on an acoustic guitar, the sound as full as if it had been electrified, but she saw no amplifier or microphone. It was a charming performance, adding an appropriately country touch to the surroundings.

The minster said his opening piece, then asked in his resonant baritone, "Who gives this woman to be married to this man?"

Her escort said, "I do," and then joined the other man and they began to sing. She recognized the song at once—"Devoted to You"—and then she realized who the two men were.

"It's the Everly Brothers," she whispered to Nolan.

"I'm glad an infant like you knows that," he whispered back. "And not cheap imitations, either."

The duo completed the song, then the minister went on with a brief ceremony—he read from a book, but if that was the

Bible, it indeed didn't lead to God intruding—and after the couple exchanged gold bands and her husband kissed her, Phil and Don performed "All I Have to Do Is Dream."

Lloyd Totter's wife Janine took the photos herself; proofs would be sent to them. Their celebrity minstrels took part in the photography. That lasted maybe four minutes.

Another wedding was coming in soon, and the Little Church of the West had no Little Reception Room of the West to offer, so a quick visit outside included Sherry hugging and kissing both brothers before they waved and headed off to a waiting limo.

Nolan said to his wife, "Elvis is dead. Those two are still alive."

Then, after Sherry retrieved her garment bag, the groom, bride and best man stood together outside the cedarwood chapel for a few minutes, talking.

She asked Nolan, "How on earth did you arrange that?"

"I didn't." He nodded over at Jon.

Who said, "They start their engagement tomorrow. I sort of got them set up backstage at the Quarter with dressing rooms and what was what. They were friendly, very down-to-earth, and I mentioned my friend was getting married today. It just sort of happened. I checked with this sentimental slob..." He nodded at Nolan. "...and he okayed it."

"And it didn't cost me a dime," Nolan said.

Jon said to Sherry, "Hey, he tried, no matter what he says. They wouldn't take anything." He got into his tux pocket and came back with an envelope, which he handed to Sherry. "These are tickets for their show Friday night at the French Quarter. My wedding present....My phone number's in there, if you two need anything."

She gave Jon a hug and offered to throw him the bouquet.

"Don't you dare," he said, and headed to his car in the Hacienda lot and the newlyweds to theirs more nearby.

The Strip a mile away had a special glow as dusk eased into night; over the mountains clouds turned orange by the sun rivaled anything Fremont Street had to offer. She glanced behind her at the little chapel, a rustic non-sequitur in this town where pioneer days were represented by neon cowboys and tourist-trap trading posts.

Soon Mr. and Mrs. Nolan were in a fireside booth for two in the Bourbon Street Grille beneath a mural of the old New Orleans plantation days of horse-drawn buggies, top hats and petticoats, as a riverboat glided by, presumably the same river that ran through their Iowa/Illinois home. No slaves in sight, but then nostalgia was selective, wasn't it?

Would she think of her wedding day and edit out the terrible events that had brought this man and her closer? Held captive as she'd been in a cabin in the woods by a dim-witted lout? How her flight for her life from the Comforts had seen her dropped to the bottom of an old abandoned well, where this man beside her had somehow managed to find her, and save her?

No, Jon in his ruffled tuxedo shirt was not the riverboat gambler. Her new husband was—only he didn't gamble, not the kind of gambling that went on in this place, anyway, and some gunslinger was mixed in there, too.

They spoke very little through her blackened Gulf shrimp and his rare prime rib, but over shared key lime pie, the conversation picked up and made an unexpected turn.

"So," he said, "if you want a kid, we better get started."

She almost choked on a tart bite. "You mean, right here in this booth? People would talk."

"Well, they might learn something. But you know what I mean."

"I don't, actually."

This subject had not come up in the context of their actually getting hitched. About six months ago—right before the Comfort incident—they had discussed some of his feelings about parenthood. He'd been reluctant.

But now here he was, saying, "I'd like to hold it at one."

"At a time?"

That made him smile. There was something endearing about it. "I mean," he said, "I think one is all I can handle. Unless you have another right away."

"Oh. This is about your age."

"As it is, I'll be in my seventies when the first kid gets out of high school. I'll be lucky to see him make it out of college."

"Or her."

"Or her. It's going to be bad enough being Grandpa Daddy, if I make it that far. And if you want to skip the parent thing, fine—if I croak early enough, you can start over with a younger man. With my blessing."

"You are one romantic son of a bitch, aren't you?"

Her flip remark got a somewhat serious answer: "I didn't used to be. You're a bad influence."

"How about I go off the pill and we just see what happens?"

"I'm game."

After the table had been cleared, they had some more of the champagne they'd been drinking, which had certainly contributed to how loose he was talking, and he said, "I'm going to make a speech."

"Okay. Wow. Well. I'm ready."

"This is a new beginning for me. A new start. That crap with the Comforts is history. I'm cool with the Chicago crowd but not beholden to them. We have a good, growing business, the two of us, which is just the straight kind of line I've been looking to get into. And I'm fond as fucking hell of you."

"Be still my heart."

"Okay. Goddamnit. I love you, Sherry. Don't hold your breath for me to say that again, ever, so make it last. But what time I've got left, I want it to be with you, and a kid of ours, too, if that's what happens, and I want to keep my nose the fuck clean. With luck the killing is behind me. Behind us."

"I love you, too."

"You went through hell because of me. Again, with luck... that was the end of it. What is it called, karma? I'm thinking all of mine has caught up with me by now."

"Like you said, with luck."

"Luck is in short supply in this town. But maybe back home we can make our own."

They went up to their room and got naked and made married person love. It wasn't as hot and heavy as when he'd had her on the floor before asking her to marry him. But it did nicely.

She got up and took a warm shower, slipped into the sexy nightie that hadn't proved necessary, and when she got back, he was deep asleep. Within a minute, so was she, dead tired from the long day and a little drunk from the bubbly.

The next thing she knew, sunlight was filtering in the filmy drapes (they didn't want you sleeping in this town) and, next to her, the bed was empty. The digital clock said 10:23 A.M. She'd really zonked out.

A note from him was on the nightstand.

Went to stretch my legs. Back by nine & catch breakfast with my child bride.

Frowning at the clock's red letters, she thought, *Not like him to be later than he said he'd be.* Knowing him, he'd woken around six, got restless and went out. Only that was four hours ago. And he was a stickler for punctuality....

But what was there to worry about here?

Then she called Jon.

5.

Nolan woke at six o'clock A.M.

Sherry, next to him, was sawing logs, which he found amusing and adorable, such a perfect little beauty doing something so human. Her snoring had never kept him awake. When he wanted to sleep, he just slept. He had done that under considerably worse conditions than being in bed next to a gorgeous young girl.

Woman, really. Wives were women, not girls.

He slipped gently from the big bed, not wanting to disturb his bride, and padded over in just his boxers to the john and closed himself in. He looked at the middle-aged man in the mirror and shook his head. Some things you just had to put up with.

Six o'clock was when he woke up back home. But six here was eight there, so in reality he'd slept in. The long day and the champagne had taken a toll, and he felt mildly disgusted with himself. After his shower, which he hoped wouldn't wake her, he toweled his hair off, not wanting to use the noisy drier, and went out to get some clothes from the dresser. Her snoring had settled down for now, but she was still deep asleep.

He wrote her a note before heading quietly out in a black polo shirt, olive shorts and sockless sneakers, looking like the vacationer he was. First order of business would be getting some fresh air, so he found his way to the pool area where he strolled through palm trees and past tropical gardens, the sundeck largely unpopulated, its chaise lounges and tables empty.

He was not one to exercise, no jogging or working out for

him. Riding a bike to nowhere was not his idea of a good use of a grown man's time. But he had, over the last several years, taken to morning walks, keeping up a good pace. He'd heard this practice called "power walking," which used to be called "race walking," and both terms seemed patently absurd to him, even if it did describe what he was doing.

No fast-clip walking out here, though. The sun, the dry heat that he found soothing, steadied his pace. Or maybe it was the palms or the shimmering water of the pools, a round one, a skinny lap one, a hot tub, all at the moment un-infringed upon by humans. When he headed back in to the casino, he maintained that easier pace. As a restaurant/nightclub man, he was interested in people. Not *as* people, of course, but customers.

He strolled through the gaming tables, overseen by another of those hanging big-headed Mardi Gras figures, this one a gaudily attired masked jester. About half the blackjack tables were doing business, only one roulette and two craps. Wherever he went, he noted the video cameras taking everything and everyone in. Now *that* was security. They should have those in the Brady Eighty parking lot.

At the Lagniappe Café, tucked under a balcony and open onto the casino floor like an airport restaurant, he got some coffee with cream and a beignet, fresh and warm. At a little round white poker chip of a table, he sat studying the patrons starting their day trying to beat the odds, confident he could sort the locals from the tourists.

While everyone was casually dressed, shorts the common denominator, the tourists wore telltale pastel—solids, floral patterns, stripes. The locals ran more to short-sleeve plaid and faded t-shirts, often advertising brands of beer that indicated their lack of taste or musical artists that announced their generation. Tourists were giddy with possibility, locals blasé about defeat.

He had just finished the hole-free doughnut when somebody said, "Hey! *There* he is."

It was Harry Bellows.

The heavyset man with the big head and little feet, in his
purple suit with gold shirt and green tie, looked a bit like one
of the casino's hanging figures had fallen. Those sharply cut
threads with their Mardi Gras colors identified executive employees of the casino—from administration to marketing. Harry
was executive host at the French Quarter.

What set Harry apart from other humans with unfortunate
physiques was a handsome face, only mildly compromised by
pockmarks and plumpness, and an affable manner. He came
over with his hand thrust out and Nolan rose to take and shake
it, trading him a smile for a grin.

Harry raised a pause palm, saying, "I'll get myself a coffee
and we'll catch up. Need a refill?"

Nolan shook his head, and Harry lowered the hand and went
over to the counter and got his coffee. He came back with a
beignet, too, and joined Nolan at the little table.

Before taking a sip or a nibble, the big head leaned forward
and asked, "Accommodations okay?"

"Great. Thanks, Harry."

"Sorry about the Honeymoon Suite. That thing gets so booked
ahead, you wouldn't believe it. And, listen, I wish I could have
made it to the Little Church thing. I was just too tied up here.
You give my apologies to Sherry, all right, buddy?"

"Don't worry about it. Sherry loves you, Harry, you know
that."

Harry knew Sherry from the Tropical, which is where Nolan
and Harry had worked together after the Outfit heat let up. The
Chicago Outfit front man had been assigned as Nolan's assistant
manager at the place, to keep an eye on him for the bosses who

had tentatively welcomed Nolan back into their fold after his years underground, heisting. Harry—who had handled the motel side—had been a real mensch in those days, really showing Nolan the motel ropes, and extolling him to Chicago.

He owed Harry for all that, and the two men became friends, if not really close. Nolan had few close friends, and no Outfit guy could be completely trusted—there was a reason why the expression wasn't honor amongst hoods.

It was no surprise that Harry worked at the French Quarter, one of the last Outfit casinos in Vegas—Bellows had never even been arrested, forget convictions. And Harry's ties to Chicago were limited to working in their legit businesses, which is what had kept him out of the Vegas "Black Book" that listed anyone with mob connections, meaning they couldn't even set foot in a casino here, much less work for one.

"You tell Sherry," Harry said, after practically inhaling the beignet, "that I have reservations for the three of us at Hugo's Cellar tonight."

The restaurant, half a flight below ground at the Four Queens, was one of the best in Vegas.

Harry held up a powdered-sugar-flecked finger, and said, "My treat," before sucking off the sweet stuff.

"Girl deserves a rose," Harry went on, "settling for a prickly character like you."

All the ladies got a rose when dining at Hugo's.

"Thanks for adding the 'l-y,' " Nolan said.

"An oversight."

"Just you tomorrow, Harry? What about Stella?"

"We're on the outs. Not divorced, not yet, anyway. I'm hoping we can get back together. We were married at the Little Church, too, you know."

Seemed like everybody was.

Stella had worked as a cocktail waitress at a casino on Fremont where Harry'd been manager, quietly representing the Outfit's interests. His host job, even with executive slapped on the front, was a step down.

"You gotta work at marriage, Nolan," Harry said. "Take it from me—you gotta take it serious. Is my advice."

"Stella still in town?"

"She is."

"Well, hell. Invite her along."

Harry grimaced. "I'll try, but don't hold out much hope."

"Oh?"

"Thing is, we're not talking right now. Nice of you to suggest it, though." He sipped coffee. "You know, your friend Jon is doing well in the Creole Showroom. Good worker. Everybody likes him. Really connects with the musicians we bring in."

Like Phil and Don, Nolan thought, saying, "Glad to hear it."

"The kid, uh...used to do scores with you, right?"

"Right."

"Not in that business anymore?"

"No. Neither of us is."

"Well, I know *you* went boy scout, but a young guy like that, lot of smarts, lot of energy, could have ideas."

"He does. Just not that kind."

"Good." The eyebrows in the handsome face rose. "They play rough out here."

"That's the rumor."

"Well!" He used a napkin, belatedly, and hauled his big self off the little chair. "I better get back to it. No rest for the you-know-what. You cool with meeting up at Hugo's tonight at eight?"

"I was cool before there *was* cool, Harry. You're a gent, by the way."

"That is *not* the rumor."

After seeing Harry lick his fingers, Nolan didn't offer a hand, just waved and smiled as the big man went off with more grace than you'd think possible. It reminded him of a time he'd seen Harry and Stella on a dance floor, and how light-footed his fat friend had been. He'd seen that kind of thing, from time to time—heavy people who were light on their feet, either a learned compensation or hidden talents.

Soon Nolan was back out prowling the casino, taking it all in. He admired the business model—Vegas, as a wise man once said, was a city built on bad math. Working the restaurant trade with its narrow margins, and clubs where trends were elusive and customers fickle, he had to envy an industry where people gave you money and you gave them pictures of lemons or just nothing at all except maybe a free drink from a pretty girl who smiles but doesn't see you unless maybe you tip.

The race and sports book, dead at the moment, held little interest for him; he liked to watch college and professional sports but betting just ruined it for him—betting the spread bored his ass. And he didn't waste much time strolling through the slots, or the video poker. Now real poker was something else, and the French Quarter had an entire room of tables. Right now only perhaps a quarter of them were seeing action, but that would change. Hold 'Em had taken over, and nobody offered draw anymore. Which was fine with him, because he was a seven-card stud man and that was still around.

The poker room was the only part of the casino that tempted him. He was thinking that maybe he'd try to steal an afternoon or late evening away from Sherry and his honeymoon to find a table with no visible sharks and plenty of fish—tourists just looking to throw back a few beers and play some friendly poker. That much thief still lurked within Nolan, "boy scout" or not.

He checked his watch in this world of no clocks and saw that it was approaching eight-thirty. Making his way lazily back toward the bank of elevators, he slowed as he moved by the row of cashiers whose cages were of the same ornamental wrought-iron as the rails of the faux-Bourbon Street balconies. Ten cages in all, only five operating at the moment.

He watched armed guards with metal boxes of cash—there was one under every game table, Nolan knew—leaving and entering what was obviously a double-locked count room. He smiled to himself, thinking it was like watching holy relics getting stowed away at the Vatican.

Moving down the central aisle of the game tables, where it was getting busier, with the same nearly equal mix of tourist and local, he would pause from time to time to take in the action. One roulette table was really cooking and he stopped for a few minutes to live vicariously.

He was doing that when two big men in the same purple suits as Harry, but minus the fat, came up alongside him and flanked him. Nolan stood over six feet, and these two both stood over Nolan. He glanced left and right; then a hand was on his either upper arm.

"Sir," said the one on his left, an African American whose breath was winter fresh and eyes were winter cold. "Would you come with us, please."

"May I ask why?"

"No," the other one said, a guy in his forties with short-cropped white hair, a trimmed white goatee and the general look of an ex-football player. Pro ball, of course.

"All right," Nolan said. "I'll go quietly."

"That's right," the white goatee said.

"Thank you, sir," the black man said.

"If you take your hands off me."

"Sir," the black man said, "we can't do that."

"I think you can. Because there'll be a scene if you don't."

"It won't last long," the white goatee said.

"Look, I'm a guest at the hotel. On my honeymoon. Why don't you check with Mr. Bellows. The executive host? My name is Nolan. Don't you have walkies or something? Or I'll wait with one of you while—"

But they hauled him off, with impressive speed—it was like watching Harry Bellows dance, feather-light—and then they were in a corridor between a café and a bank of cheap slots, a featureless shaft that led to an unmarked doorway that he did not want to go through. So he stuck his leg in front of the white guy hauling him, sending him tumbling, while the black guy kept moving forward, as Nolan held his ground, using the surprise to pull his arms free.

He kicked the white guy in the ass, foot-of-the-shoe hard, and sent him the rest of the way down, like the bastard dived into a swimming pool whose water had suddenly froze, outstretched arms swimming in nothing. The black guy swiveled and Nolan slammed a fist into his belly, but those fucking abs were rock hard, and the next blow Nolan threw, at the guy's chin, got swatted away like an annoying gnat.

Then the other guy was up and they were hauling him again, very fucking fast, and were through the door into the room, a concrete chamber just big enough to echo. The black guy held him while the white guy punched him in the belly and various other places, chest, ribs, kidneys, but staying away from his face. When he eventually got hauled out of here, they would not want his face messed up. That might alarm the paying customers.

Now and then, the black guy would say, "That's enough, Vin."

"Fuck it is, Leo," Vin would say.

Rinse. Repeat.

Finally Nolan got slammed into a chair and he felt the handcuffs go on his wrists and heard the metallic snap. His legs were free but he couldn't get at either man, again with the black guy on his left and the white on his right.

He was barely conscious, his head hanging, when Leo turned out to have a walkie after all, and used it to say, "We have him downstairs. Gave us some trouble."

Nolan had nothing clever to say. He was just sitting there hurting all over his midsection, wondering if any ribs were broken and also trying not to cry, not wanting to satisfy that white prick. The black guy was a better sort, but he would gladly kick the fucker's teeth out, given half a chance.

While they waited for whoever was coming, Nolan did his best to take in the surroundings. He was sitting facing the door he'd been dragged through. His chair was metal. A metal picnic-type table was to his left, nothing on it. Maybe it was for emptying out a toolbox of such handy items as hammers, drills, chisels, nail guns. Do it yourself stuff. The walls were cream-color padded canvas, tufted like a leather chair. A padded cell, of sorts. But really just elaborately soundproofed.

No responsible casino employee could beat the shit out of a guy and allow the patrons out there to hear the unpleasantness rising over the bells and whistles of them losing money.

Nolan flicked a glance over his shoulder. A door was back there, punched out of the padded cell. On the outside would be the parking lot. Still a possibility of a beat-up subject being seen by a customer while getting hauled out. Of course, if a car was backed up close, and its trunk lid was up, especially after dark, the subject could be dropped in and driven out for a tour of a stretch of desert and maybe an already dug hole. That would work for already dead subjects, too. Wouldn't matter which end of the trip you died on, the hole was waiting.

Waiting for all of us, he thought, somewhat deliriously.

For the next four minutes or so, nobody beat on him.

The man who came through the door was so important, he wasn't wearing the purple, gold and green ensemble. Instead he wore a gray sports jacket, a salmon shirt and white tie, his slacks and shoes white, too; that outfit hadn't cost any more than a second car. He had a cigarette in a holder in his right hand. His bland, blond handsomeness was flawed only by a too-high forehead. If he'd been any smoother, he'd have been a Ken doll.

With unimpressed eyes and a trace of a smile, the new arrival walked over and planted himself before Nolan, though not close enough to get himself kicked. He had a draw from the cigarette-in-holder. He let out smoke forming what was nearly a question mark. Good trick.

"Mr. Nolan," he said, in a voice that was midrange and unthreatening. "You were recognized."

With Leo at his right, and Vin on his left, Nolan nonetheless risked saying, "Got a commendation, you mean?"

The casino man chuckled. "Not in that sense of recognized. You're familiar with the so-called 'Eye-in-the-Sky.' "

"No. I'm just some dumb asshole."

"We have quite an elaborate set-up, Mr. Nolan—electronically state of the art. We have you on tape, if you're interested."

"If this is a chance to buy a tape of myself on vacation, I'll pass."

He took in more smoke, then let it out. "I assume you know that our parent company is in Illinois. Some of our employees hail from there. The Windy City?"

"Nobody from there calls it that," Nolan said.

Half a smile. "I'm not *from* there. But, as I say, my employers are. One of my people, who does hail from those parts, says your name is Nolan. And he informs me that you are a thief. A very successful one, well-regarded in certain circles."

"I was. More recently I worked for your employers myself. Check with Harry Bellows. He worked with me at one of their places. *For* me, actually."

The casino man frowned. Then he turned to Leo. "Get Harry on the walkie. Have him join us."

Thank God, Nolan thought.

Then said, "Do you know Felix in Chicago?"

"If I do?"

"Call him, too. I have my own restaurant and nightclub now. In the Iowa/Illinois Quad Cities. I'm out of the game. Strictly straight."

"…If so, we've made a mistake."

"Tell me about it."

"Maybe you can explain why you were…casing the joint?"

Nolan laughed. It hurt and he stopped.

The casino man was saying, "Eyeballing every security camera? Checking out the table games? The poker room? The cashier cages? The counting room?"

"Oh, right. I checked out the counting room. When nobody was looking, I ran in there and dove into the piles of money like Uncle Scrooge and tossed hundreds in the air. Just lolled the fuck around."

Vin had a fist ready and boy did he want to use it, but the casino man said, "No," then to Nolan said, "Why reconnoiter, then?"

Nolan shrugged. That hurt, too.

"Habit," he said.

The casino man frowned. "Let's have a better answer."

"Jesus, man. No thief except a fucking fool thinks there's any way to knock over a casino. Fort Knox, maybe, in James Bond. Joints like this, in the real world? No fucking way."

A knock came to the door. The casino man nodded to Vin, who went and answered it. A concerned-looking Harry was there with Leo.

"Mr. Briggs," Harry said, from the corridor, "this is a horrible misunderstanding."

Vin returned to Nolan's side and the casino man went out and talked with Harry in the hall, door open. Harry gestured toward Nolan, looking very upset, and now and then Nolan picked up on a word or phrase: "...for years...tight with Felix... straight...stand-up guy...."

The casino man came back in, shutting the door on Harry out there. Planting himself in front of Nolan, he said, "We made an honest mistake, Mr. Nolan. Can we put this behind us?"

Translation: Do I have to have you killed to make this go away?

Nolan said, "What did that guy say at the end of *Some Like It Hot*?"

"Nobody's perfect," the casino man said. Then to Vin: "Unlock the cuffs."

Vin was doing that when the casino man leaned in and asked, "Can we make this right?"

"Me burying Vin in the desert would be a start," Nolan said. Then he grinned at Vin. "Kidding."

The casino man helped Nolan get to his feet. "I'm Jack Briggs. You need anything here, anybody gives you trouble, you mention my name."

He handed Nolan his card.

"Work and home," Briggs said. "Day or night."

Then the casino man was gone.

Nolan looked at the two security thugs and said, "By the way, fellas…no goddamn hard fucking feelings."

He got out of there, hoping Sherry was still sleeping in. If he'd caused her any worry, he might have to hurt somebody, even if nobody was perfect.

6.

Daniel Clifford, who'd had his last name legally changed from Comfort over twenty-five years ago, had in his formative years learned many tricks of his older brother Cole's trade.

In the intervening decades the small mustached man with thinning dark hair and the sharp-featured oval face had done nothing particularly dishonest, certainly not that would have been of interest to law enforcement or, say, a bank examiner. Still, that early brotherly training may have been why, after all this time, he'd had no compunction about originating several modest false loans and stealing the proceeds.

The false loans he felt would likely get past the bank examiner, at least initially. But not the customer loan payments he'd used to pay back those fictitious loans, which he'd intended to restore but time and opportunity had conspired against him. Now he was in the position of having to turn to the mother he loved and loathed, avoided and feared.

On the day he'd gone to visit her, she had been ready for him.

Sitting at that table over beer and peanuts in her hellishly messy kitchen, he had responded to her insane demand that he bring back Nolan's head by saying, "I'm not Cole. I'm not up to this. Maw, I wouldn't begin to know how to go about it."

"Take a look in the basket, boy," she'd said with a cackle. With her round face and gray curls, she looked like what Betty Boop might have grown up into, if Betty had a really hard life.

He removed the lid from the woven repository intended for the results of a decapitation that seemed both absurd and abstract to him. There was, at its interlaced base, a spiral notebook that a child might take to the fourth grade. She wiggled a finger at him, indicating he should take the notebook out. He did and she snatched it from him.

As she sat facing him, the immense woman in the muumuu opened the cover of the child's notebook with a steady adult hand. She turned the thing toward him, fanned open, revealing ruled paper. The first page was filled with his brother Cole's familiar cramped but entirely legible handwriting. Tucked in a side pocket was a well-stuffed white #10 envelope.

"These are your brother's notes about where this piece of shit lives," she said. "Things and stuff Cole observed checkin' out the place, inside and out. There's diagrams and such, too."

She flipped pages and demonstrated. The diagrams of the house were surprisingly careful and complete, including the layout of the rooms on the first floor and the finished basement.

"Now, the S.O.B. has an alarm, but he doesn't turn it on at night," she said, "or anyway dint back when Cole was casing him. The alarm's only for when he and his gal go out, and it's possible they don't turn it on then—probably mostly use it when they're gonna be away overnight or some such. You should slip in there in the wee hours. Get Nolan's attention by popping that bitch in the bonnet."

Daniel blinked. "*What* bitch?"

"One he lives with. He's another one of you dirty old men that likes a young piece of tail."

Now she had him murdering *two* people!

And her denigrating Heather like that struck Daniel as gratuitous, but he said nothing. His mind was whirling with the idea of killing a woman.

Maw said, "Best familiarize yourself with her ahead of time."

She flipped back to the front of the notebook and plucked

out the letter-sized envelope, untucked its flap and dumped out a dozen or so photos, Polaroids, many of them angles on Nolan's house, but some indoors too. She sorted through and found one of an attractive woman with blonde-tipped light brown hair wearing a leopard-print winter coat and black leather high-heel boots. The babe was getting out of a dark blue Nissan 300 ZX in the driveway.

Nice, he thought, one word covering both the girl and the wheels. He'd forgotten briefly that she was one of his intended victims.

Maw was saying, "Now if the bastard's got more jumpy after bumpin' heads with Coleman, he may leave the alarm on these days. But not to worry—your brother found the code jotted on a slip of paper in the bitch's purse."

"Purse-snatching," Daniel said dryly, "seems a little beneath my big brother."

"It was the *girl* he snatched," Maw said, irritatedly. "Purse came along with her."

"Surely that code'll have been changed by now," Daniel said, lighting up a fresh Kent with his Bic. "If this Nolan got the best of Cole, he must be smart...and dangerous as hell."

"Oh he is," she admitted, "but he won't see you comin'. And, anyway, he's gone straight and that makes a body soft. Still, even with that bitch dead in bed next to him, you'll likely have to put some bullets in him, 'fore he tells you what he done with Coleman."

Daniel's head was spinning, but he managed to say, "What if he *has* changed the alarm code, Maw? I mean, he's surely no fool."

"Your brother's notes say that alarm don't go to the cops, just some local security firm, on the Iowa side of the river. Nolan's house is on the Illinois side."

"What makes you think they don't patrol both?"

She beamed. "*Now* you're thinkin', son. Go in there no earlier than two in the morning. When they're in bed and dead to the world and ready to get deader."

"…Okay."

She curled a finger at him like she was pointing out which apple Snow White should eat. "Bastard always goes in around back. Through the glass doors of the fixed-up basement. The alarm wires the front door and the door from the garage and a couple of windows, and those glass doors downstairs. You have thirty seconds to turn off the alarm usin' a keypad."

"How am I supposed to get in there? Breaking in the front, even in early morning hours, I could be seen or heard. Breaking plate glass in back, I could easily wake them up."

"You don't have to break glass to get in, son. Don't you remember your trainin'?"

"What training?"

She leaned in, confidential, as if the place might be bugged —this kitchen certainly might be, in a different way. "When you went out on jobs with Sam and Cole as a fresh-faced squirt? Cole thought you had a knack. You was only sixteen when you put a bullet in that security guard's brain. Back then I thought you had potential. Maybe you still do. Maybe you got the stones for what needs doing, and can earn the right to take over the family business."

That he'd killed a man once was not Daniel's proudest moment. It had a lot to do with why he'd rejected the life his brothers would gladly have made him part of.

Yet Maw approving of him touched something in him, no matter how much he tried to deny it to himself.

From a muumuu pocket, she took an object that at first he thought was an eyeglasses case. She thunked it down before him, between the ashtray and his can of beer—a well-worn black leather pouch. She unzipped it, flipped it open, and revealed facing pockets holding five lock picks and a tension wrench on either side.

"Bring back memories?" Maw asked.

It did. A gift on his fifteenth birthday from his brother Cole. Daniel had left the tool-kit pouch behind when he went off to community college, leaving his mother weeping at the front door.

"You hung onto it," he said.

"Always been a sentimental soul," she said. "Now, you can't be drivin' your own car on this jaunt."

"I suppose I could rent…"

"No! Use the brains God and your Maw gave you!" She reached in another muumuu pocket and brought back a wad of cash held together with a rubber band. "Four grand—take it. You'll go to a St. Lou used car dealer Cole did business with. He'll give you papers and sign over the pink slip. Store your car there while you're gone."

He was lighting up another Kent. "What if a cop stops me?"

"Don't give one occasion to. Can't you manage to stay under the speed limit and not run any stop signs, or are you just a hopeless asshole?"

"But what if one catches me breaking in to that house?"

She shrugged. "You'll have the piece I'm gonna give you."

He hadn't used a gun in years. "And shoot a *cop*?"

"Or go to jail. Probably prison, in your case, 'cause your shenanigans at the bank will come to light. Wanna be some jigaboo's butt boy? Hard choices to make in this life, son."

His eyes were tearing up. "Maw…how can you ask this of me?"

For a moment her expression softened, then hardened.

"You're all I got left, son. I'm just an old woman with no one else to turn to."

"But you're asking too much...."

Maw reached over and patted his cheek, then the pat turned into a gentle slap—but a slap.

She said, "Am I? Do your family proud, boy, and all of this will be yours." She gestured around the filthy cluttered kitchen; through the open archway onto the living room, from their places on the wall, the King and the Duke looked on.

Daniel knew his mother's promise was not as absurd as it might seem—tens of thousands were stashed in this old dump. And that fencing business really would be incredibly lucrative....

"I'm not cutting his head off," Daniel said firmly. "Killing him is where I draw the line."

"No!" She slammed a fist on the table and the beers and ashtray and peanuts in their bowl all jumped. So did Daniel. "I want his goddamn head. *I want it!*"

Daniel swallowed. "Well, I'm not doing it while he's alive. The blood would..."

Maw haw-haw-hawed. "It would be like Old Faithful kickin' in!"

"That's right, and I'd look like Carrie at the prom."

"...Who? Where?"

"He's got to be dead already. If he's dead, there'll be no red gusher. And I won't have to take a shower in a dead man's house, and steal some of his clothes, before I leave. I'll bring you your trophy, but only on those terms. Take it or leave it, Maw."

She grinned; some red peanut skin was stuck to one of her front teeth. "Daniel, maybe you have some spine at that. Fine. Long as, 'fore you put one 'tween his eyes, you make him know you come to fetch his head for me. Fair enough?"

"I can live with that," Daniel said.

Several days later, in the light pink-walled master bedroom of an under-furnished home so new it still smelled of construction chemicals, Daniel in a polo shirt and Bermuda shorts and sandals was packing the gun his mother had given him. He'd already packed the leather-sheathed machete his mother had given him—where on earth had she found that? Home Shopping Network?

The .22 automatic, a Browning, had attached to it a surprisingly short perforated noise suppressor, extending the barrel to not much more than seven inches. He had a windbreaker, which he'd already packed away in the suitcase, with a pocket that it would just fit into. In some of his underwear he squirreled away a box of .22 ammo he'd purchased at the new Walmart Supercenter there in O'Fallon.

His young wife's voice from the bedroom doorway, high-pitched and sexy and a little stupid, asked, "What ya doin' there, handsome?"

He got the ammo stowed just in time as she scooted up beside him.

"I'm, uh, packing," he said, quite used to answering dumb obvious questions from her.

She was small, in terms of height—under five foot. She was large, in terms of bosom. With almost no waist and a boyish bottom, the tits were the thing, and on every day of his life since they met at the Three Fountains in Gaslight Square, he had wanted those puppies in his face and his life. Some men dreamed of owning a yacht; he was quite content with motorboating.

Even burdened with alimony for both previous wives, and child support for one, Daniel knew that at last he'd found the right woman, a female worth whatever the freight proved to be. And she was shorter than he was, too.

Her hair was an explosion of platinum and her big baby-blue

eyes lived in a face cuter than Shirley Temple's at ten. She was a good little homemaker, a decent cook, and did the laundry, with none of that feminist baloney in the mix. Her only fault, if you could call it that, was a yen for expensive things—clothes and shoes particularly, and she was planning to fill this new house with the best pricey things Goedeker's Furniture had to offer.

At the moment she was wearing a very short blue-jeans mini-skirt and a gray tank top with the words TOTALLY AWESOME angled across a palm tree and mountain sunset to which her breasts were lending a 3-D effect.

"Why can't you take me along, Daddy?" she asked. "I'm not working or anything."

And she wasn't. When they got married, she quit her bartending job.

"It's a boring banker's conference in a boring town," he said. "I wouldn't put you through that."

Actually, he was taking a week of his vacation time at the bank.

"I could just stay in the hotel and watch TV and then when you got back, we could go to some nice restaurant and then find someplace fun to party."

She liked to drink and dance. Pot now and then, too, but never coke or anything harder. Not that kind of girl. Really just a nice, fun-loving kid.

"Next time," he said.

She pulled the tank top off and unleashed those monsters. She had a bikini tan that emphasized the size of them, the nipples popping from aureoles bigger than his first wife's breasts. She went around and crawled up on the bed's pink satin bedspread and lay on her back next to the open suitcase that had a gun and a machete she didn't know about in it.

"Come up here, big boy," she said.

He scrambled out of his shorts and jockeys, which had already been tenting, but left his polo shirt on as he got into a familiar position, straddling her. She stuffed a doubled pillow behind her head and took his stiff-to-bursting dick in her mouth, sucking the tip but then licking all around to provide some moisture. Then he eased away and slid himself between those casabas. She watched him, amused, as she pressed herself around him to give plenty of tightness in the passageway as he thrust, and in under a minute he had covered her throat, filled its hollow, with white.

Sex between the man and wife ran to this kind of thing more often than more traditional coupling. He suspected Heather liked the relative lack of fuss and muss, and it was always over quick. She snatched some Kleenex from the box at the ready on the nightstand, and dabbed at herself, her baby face cooing, "*Now* can I come along?"

As he climbed off, exhausted, precious bodily fluids drained, he said, "No, baby, no. Not this time."

Her big eyes got bigger—she seemed astonished her bribe hadn't worked. Her right hand grabbed one breast and her left hand grabbed the other. "You don't want *these* along? Are you fucking nuts?"

"I'm, uh, fucking nuts about you, babe," he said, availing himself of several tissues, "but this is strictly business. Really is."

She climbed off the bed and stormed out, grabbing up her tank top as she went. "Well, don't bother calling me while you're gone! No phone sex for you, you big meanie!"

Six hours and a few minutes later, Daniel was checking in at the Starlite Motel on the 19th Street Hill in Moline, Illinois, its impressive neon sign dating to 1960 or so. This was a traveling businessman's hotel, clean and comfortable and recently refurbished, close to downtown; but for locals it was also a no-tell motel, where cash and "John Smith" (or the like) was all you needed to check in.

The Starlite had been recommended to him by a typical used car salesman—clip-on tie, skinny, hyper—at the St. Louis address Maw had provided, only the guy wasn't all that typical, considering what his specialty was, as explained by Maw.

"Well," she'd told Daniel, "ol' Eddie bids at auction on wrecked cars and scavenges everything usable off to sell for parts and scrap metal. But he holds onto the VIN numbers. Then he orders up a ride from his car boosting connections— same make, model, and year. Switches the stolen buggy's VIN with the new one and sells the cooled-off hot car at a premium to his special clientele."

Which is why Daniel, chain-smoking up a storm, had driven to the Quad Cities in a 1976 Dodge Dart that had been maybe $3,200 new, but had cost him, twelve years later, about the same. Medium blue, with a radio and air conditioner, it was everything he wanted in a car on this trip, especially nondescript.

After checking in at the Starlite, Daniel drove to Harold's on the Rock in Moline, an old-fashioned steakhouse in a park-like setting on the Rock River. There he consumed a lobster supper with garlic salad and baked potato and two vodka gimlets—he wanted to feel loose, even get a little buzzed, as he was uncomfortable with the task ahead. The food tasted fantastic and he felt very relaxed, but then on his way out, after paying for the meal, he paid again by stopping in the men's room and puking it all up.

He knew from his brother's notes that Nolan usually got home around eleven P.M. As Maw suggested, Daniel wanted him and the woman to be sleeping when he entered. To do the distasteful deed of shooting the female in the head and then putting bullets into each leg of the slumbering man, presumably waking him up.

Jesus. Could he really do that? He thought about Maw's money. He thought about Heather's titties.

At around two A.M., Daniel guided the Dart into the small, exclusive housing development. Nolan's house was a low, rambling ranch-style with a big manicured yard and trees to right and left and looming in back. No house directly across the way. The next-door neighbor wasn't close; neither was the thoroughfare you turned off. Nicely secluded for Daniel's purposes. From the look of the place, the guy had money.

The development itself was just another seven houses on a cul-de-sac. No lights were on in any of the homes, though streetlamps pooled the night with light. He wouldn't park here on the street. Even with everyone in the neighborhood in bed, he didn't want to attract attention. He left the Dart one street over, realizing that after Nolan was dead, going back for the car and the basket and the machete in the trunk would be a necessary evil. Walking back in his windbreaker, navy polo and tan khakis wouldn't be overly suspicious; walking along with a basket and a machete would be.

Turned out maybe he could have risked it. Traffic was almost nonexistent. But when a police car rolled by, he peed a little.

No light was on in Nolan's house. Not one. Daniel was ready for that, a small flashlight in his left windbreaker pocket, the silenced .22 in the right one, making a big lump he hoped wasn't too fucking noticeable. He walked up the driveway and looked in the windows of the double garage. The woman's ZX was in there, but Nolan's silver Trans Am wasn't.

Could Nolan not be home at two in the morning? Out late, or away…?

And what would Daniel do with the girl, if Nolan wasn't there? Go ahead and kill her?

But he'd come this far.

Daniel paused for a moment, wondering whether to go in the front or back way. Picking the lock on the street side—even at this hour and with no house directly opposite—carried risks, as he'd said to his mother. Going in back would be safer, though it provided more opportunity to make a noise and alert an inhabitant.

He walked around the side of the house and onto the patio, then got the lock picks from his right pants pocket. He'd practiced at home on a pin tumbler lock, and was glad to see the glass door back here had one of those.

In under thirty seconds, he was in, feeling good about his success with the lock picks—like riding a bike! That feeling was gone as fast as it came, because in another thirty seconds that alarm would go off. When his pocket flash's beam found the keypad at right on the nearby wall, as Cole's notes indicated, several red lights were flashing. He entered the code and a single green light came on, meaning the alarm was now unarmed.

Then, after a few moments of relief, he realized he was standing in darkness in the house of one dangerous son of a bitch. He switched the flash to his left hand and got out the silenced .22 with his right, and let the narrow beam guide his way around the basement, which had a bar and a pool table and a TV area, but also an open stairway. Up he went, slowly, carefully, doing his best not to make a sound. Knowing the layout of the house from his brother's diagrams, he paused at the top to listen for anyone who might still be awake—nothing. And no lights were on under the doorways of the hallway that led to the bedroom where Nolan and the girl would be, if both were home.

But without that Trans Am in the garage, Daniel wondered if he shouldn't just peek in that bedroom, and if the girl was in there sleeping without her man next to her, just slip back out and try again tomorrow around this time.

He turned the knob and eased the door open; the wall-to-wall carpet made that even smoother and almost soundless.

Though he'd guided himself through the house with the little flashlight, he did not raise the beam, as a window let in enough moonlight and some street light, too.

But the bed was made.

Not only no Nolan, no girl.

Methodically, with the silenced weapon in his right hand and the flash in the left, he checked every room in the house.

Nothing.

Then he did it again, switching lights on in each room, giving them a thorough look, then shutting them off and moving on to the next. Throughout this process he had a cigarette going. He went through three Kents going through the house, not searching, just eyeballing.

Finally he went into the kitchen and turned a light on over the sink before opening the fridge. He selected a bottle of Coors and twisted off the cap and leaned against the counter, where he'd rested the weapon, the flashlight already tucked away. That was when he noticed it.

A slip of notepaper near the phone had the word VEGAS in big confident cursive, and underneath three items:

> *flights* ✔
> *hotel* ✔
> *chapel* ✔

No flight numbers, no specific hotel or chapel, and no dates.

But that explained it.

The house was empty.

Almost.

7

When Nolan got back to their hotel suite, he found Sherry pacing, her long blonde hair bouncing, legs flashing; she was in a bright floral baby doll dress that made him wonder if she needed a spanking. Or something.

She froze and her hands turned into fists.

"Where have you *been*?" she demanded, frowning, really cross with him, then ran over and flew into his arms and hugged him desperately. Since her abduction, six months ago, he'd noticed she tended toward overreacting.

She squeezed him so hard, burying her face in his chest, that he said, "Oww."

She drew away, frowning again but this time in concern. "Are you all right?"

A knock came at the door, just behind him—he'd barely stepped into the room—and he eased Sherry away, motioned her to one side.

Quickly he went to the dresser and got out his Smith & Wesson Model 10 with its four-inch barrel from between folded clothes. He didn't have to check it—he knew it was loaded and ready.

The knock repeated, and a voice said, "Sherry? It's Jon."

Nolan let some air out, then opened the door and Jon grinned seeing him, but the younger man's brows went up as he took in the revolver in his host's hand, lowered though it was now.

"Didn't you see the 'Do Not Disturb'?" Nolan asked, but half-smiled and gestured his friend in and shut the door.

Jon, in jeans and a gray t-shirt with an orange Elvis Costello figure on it, joined Nolan and Sherry in a semi-circle, as if they were planning the next play in the big game.

"Sherry called me," Jon said, nodding at her, "saying you went missing."

"That's maybe overstated," Nolan said, putting the .38 back in his suitcase, "but something happened, yeah. Why don't we get lunch here somewhere. I'll fill both of you in."

In the French Marketplace Café—with its expected wrought iron, red brick and hanging ferns—the trio settled into a corner booth, Sherry in the middle. Basin Street jazz poured in gently over the sound system but could not overcome the ding-ding-ding din from the casino the restaurant opened onto. They ordered lunch portions of Fried Shrimp and Grits (Nolan), gumbo and a shrimp Po' Boy (Jon), and a Creole Caesar salad (Sherry). While they waited for their food, sipping at Long Island iced teas, Nolan told them of his adventure.

Jon laughed when Nolan got to the part about the casino manager grilling him.

"Happy I'm amusing you," Nolan said.

"Oh," Jon said, "I don't find it funny they pounded you like a minute steak. I'm sympathetic as hell about that."

"I'm touched."

He laughed some more. "But what did you *think* they'd think? You walk around studying their operation, doing everything but taking notes. *Of course* they thought you were casing the joint!"

Nolan grunted and said, "Who's dumb enough to try heisting a casino?"

Jon shrugged, sipped his drink. "I dunno. Frank Sinatra and Dean Martin in the movies? Maybe they saw who it was and thought you had one mountain left to climb."

Sherry was listening to all this, alternately horrified and amused.

When Nolan's tale had been told, she asked him, "Are you all right? Do you need to see a doctor?"

Her husband shook his head.

Jon said, "He just needs to be held."

Nolan glowered at him, but was hiding a smile, not very well.

"I wonder if we should check out of this place," Sherry said, looking around like they were in a haunted house. "Maybe we can find a hotel where hospitality isn't spelled hostility."

Jon said, "Right, where your hubby can stroll around and case the joint and take another beating."

Nolan raised a palm, as if silencing the class. "First, Jon is right."

"What?" the younger man said, blinking like he'd had water thrown in his face.

"I was a dope," Nolan admitted. "Walking around like I was memorizing the place. This is a Chicago-run joint. Not surprising somebody recognized me. Blame is mine."

Jon, not joking now, said, "Those two security thugs you mixed it up with—any possibility they might make a hobby out of you, in their spare time?"

"I wish they would," he said, not kidding.

Sherry touched his hand. "We don't want that kind of thing on this trip, do we? This is a boy–girl thing, not boys-will-be-boys. I mean, it's our honeymoon, for crying out loud. Look, this is a nice enough place, but let's go somewhere else."

"Yeah," Jon said. "You could go to the Flamingo and case *that* joint. Be sure to tell them Bugsy was a friend of yours."

Nolan did something that amazed the other two: he laughed.

Then he said, "What you two fail to realize is that I managed something rare in this town."

Jon asked, "Which is?"

"Yeah," Sherry said, looking narrow-eyed at him, "which is what?"

He shrugged rather grandly. "Beat the house. Five will get you ten—and I say this as a man who doesn't bet on just *anything* that comes down the pike—our rooms…our meals, everything… will be comped."

"Speaking of meals," Jon said.

Their food was being placed before them, after which the conversation became limited to how they were enjoying this good lunch, and some talk about how the afternoon would be spent. A deal was negotiated between bride and groom where Sherry would go to the Fashion Show Mall with a credit card and Nolan would look for tourists to fleece in the poker room. As for Jon, he would have to get back, literally, to the drawing board.

They were having dessert—Nolan and Sherry sharing sweet potato pecan pie, Jon a serving of praline bread pudding he wasn't sharing with anybody—when a male voice called out good-naturedly, "*Hey! There* you are! Been *looking* everywhere for you…"

You might expect the fat man with the big handsome head and small feet to waddle over, but he was graceful, Nolan's old pal Harry Bellows. In his purple suit, gold shirt and green tie, he stood out garishly even in the restaurant's self-conscious New Orleans look.

"Sherry!" Harry said, who of course had known her at the Tropical, and he nodded at Jon. "You are a still a stone-cold stunner, young lady! The showgirls in this town better mind their p's and q's….You folks enjoy your lunch?"

With smiles and nods, they all indicated they had.

"Well," Harry said with a grandiose gesture, "it's courtesy of the French Quarter Casino and Hotel."

The big man slid in next to Nolan, who made room, which took a little doing. Harry leaned close, his voice lowering to a near-confidential tone. "Nolan, Nolan, Nolan, old friend, I am *so* damn sorry. I don't know what to say....Are you all right? I...I'm sorry things got a little out of hand this morning."

"A little."

"I did my best to curtail it, as you know. Do you need medical attention?"

"Only if we have a second slice of pie." Nolan put a hand on Harry's purple coat sleeve. "Harry, don't worry yourself. Your man Briggs was very gracious about everything. But I had the feeling..." He shrugged.

"What? *What*, man?"

"Felt like he would like to make it up to us. In some way. Some fashion."

Harry raised his hands as if he was being held up, which wasn't far from the truth. "Well, your stay is being *comped*, of course! And that includes any meals at the Quarter. *All* that's on us."

"Very generous, Harry."

The handsome face swiveled to Sherry. "But we're going to make it up to you, too, little lady. I talked to Mr. Briggs—who Nolan met, he's the top man here—about how disappointed you were to miss out on that Honeymoon Suite. Well, actually we have several of those, and one of them—in our overflow facility out in back—will be available tonight."

Sherry began, "That's not—"

"Thank you," Nolan said to his one-time associate, "that's a hell of a generous gesture, and we're pleased to accept."

Harry beamed. "Good! And if you'd like to extend your stay, at the hotel's expense, that suite is available through the coming weekend."

Nolan shrugged. "No downside to a nice long honeymoon. We're not rushing to get back for anything."

"Fred can cover for us," Sherry said, thinking it through.

Harry was saying, "And at our front desk, by late afternoon, your keys will be ready, with directions to your new suite. A bellman will move you. Now. Anything else I can do for you?"

Another shrug from Nolan. "I'm going to play a little poker this afternoon. Can the house stand me to a couple thousand in chips?"

After an almost imperceptible pause, Harry blurted, "Absolutely! Two thousand enough?"

"Four would be even better."

A nod as if from the Pope. "Four it is....Now, don't forget—we dine at Hugo's tonight at eight. Uh, would your friend like to join us, too?"

"Working tonight," Jon said. "Backstage."

"Too bad," Harry said, almost convincingly.

Nolan asked, "Is Stella going to make it?"

"Yes," he said, and sighed. "The estranged wife has deigned to spend time with her worthless husband. She's always liked you, Nolan. You be sure to tell her what a great guy I am. Put in the good word."

"I'll do that."

Harry squeezed out of the booth before he got squeezed any further by Nolan. He went away on his tiny light feet, smiling over his shoulder and waving.

"Nice guy, Harry," Nolan said.

"You're unbelievable," Jon said, smiling, shaking his head. "You really *did* beat the house."

"If you'd taken what I did from those clowns," he said, "you might have gone after more....So, babe? You like the sound of that honeymoon suite?"

"Well, yes," she said. "Sounds more private—we won't have to walk through the casino to get there. But what's 'overflow facility' mean?"

Jon said, "Strictly hotel rooms, no casino stuff. Not even a slot, no lobby proper. Built last year when the casino started taking off."

Nolan asked, "What can we expect?"

"Three floors of 'fantasy suites,' so that should be fun. It's a nice lure to pull more guests in. People tend to gamble where they stay, you know."

"Not having enough rooms available," Nolan said thoughtfully, "is what killed Ben Siegel at the Flamingo, opening weekend." He shrugged. "Of course, bullets finished the job later in L.A."

"And here the poor guy," Jon said archly, "was just trying to leave a life of crime behind and go straight."

Sherry frowned. "Is that true?"

Nolan shook his head. "Siegel was stealing from other mobsters. Skimming. Never a good plan, except when the boys skim from themselves, to send tax-free money home. Lot of that goes on in this town. Including right under this roof, you can bet."

"You're sort of skimming from them yourself, aren't you?" Jon asked, with half a smile. "Getting comped for rooms and meals and handed all those free poker chips?"

Nolan shook his head. "That's not skimming. I put my hand out and they filled it, 'cause they wanted to. Because they fucked up by working me over. I still have friends in Chicago, you know. And I have a reputation for getting even when somebody pulls shit like that."

"Do tell," Jon said deadpan.

Sherry excused herself to use the restroom, and Jon scooted over to where she'd been sitting and leaned toward his friend.

"Look," Jon said, "there's something I wanted to talk to you about. But not in front of the missus."

"What you started to tell me on the phone?"

"Right." Quickly Jon explained about his plan to buy Neon

Comics and use the shop to underwrite his cartooning career. And the need for thirty grand to do it. "Now, I'm not asking you to invest. Not hitting you up for a loan and certainly not a handout."

"What *are* you asking?"

Jon swallowed. He almost whispered, "One last job. One last score."

"...You have something in mind?"

"No, that's your department. *Not* heist a casino, that's for damn sure."

Nolan raised a palm. "Setting up scores was never really my deal. Planner's department, more like it."

"My uncle's dead."

"Right. Got himself killed in this game. One last job? That ends one of two ways—*another* last job and another and another...or fucking dead. Thirty K for just your end means a pretty big score. No."

"What if I come up with the right thing?"

"No. I don't do that anymore. I just got married, remember? My legit business is doing fine. I don't need the grief or the money. Maybe we can figure out some other way I can help you."

Sherry was heading over from the ladies'.

"What trouble are you boys getting yourselves into?" she asked, seeing Jon in her place in the booth. She took his.

"None," Nolan said.

"Catching up," Jon said.

The check came and Nolan signed his name and room number to it, adding a generous tip.

Forcing a smile, Jon headed off, saying he'd see the newlyweds at the Everly Brothers concert tomorrow night.

Nolan ushered Sherry outside and into a cab to take her to the mall, which was maybe a ten-minute ride. Then he headed back to the suite to shower and freshen up from that little morning workout with Leo and Vin. He left the room in a Quad Cities River Bandits t-shirt with raccoon logo and brown polyester slacks and sandals, this time with socks, to add an air of unsophistication. Downstairs, in the gift shop, he bought a hokey FRENCH QUARTER baseball cap and snugged it on, completing the look.

Tourist season for Nolan should have required a hunting license.

At the end of his afternoon session in the poker room, he was up three grand, plus the four grand the casino had comped him. Not a bad haul, and nobody spotted him for a hustler, or— if they did—chose not to make an issue of it.

On his way back to the suite, to get himself into real clothes, he stopped at the gift shop again and arranged for flowers to be delivered to the honeymoon suite in the fantasy-suites building. That was when he saw Vin in his purple suit heading into the men's room.

On a whim, Nolan trailed after.

Seven stalls and seven urinals and seven sinks, and business seemed steady if a little slow. He knew under these circumstances getting Vin alone would be tricky, but he might have a shot, since the man wasn't pissing. That meant, by means of shrewd deduction, the security thug was in one of the shitters.

Nolan smiled.

He ambled along checking under each stall's door to tally the occupants. Three stalls were empty. Four were a temporary home to patrons of the casino, including (and this made Nolan smile again) an actual apparently genuine manifestation of socks and sandals. Some people.

The space below only one stall door betrayed purple pants on the part of a pooper.

Nolan waited. The smells back here in Latrine Alley added up to a bouquet not likely to rival that of the flowers he'd just ordered for his bride. He waited. He waited some more.

And a flush.

When the stall door opened, Nolan forced it in and into the occupant, then butted it closed again as Vin stumbled backward, startled. Grabbing the purple lapels, Nolan pushed him back, the crapper catching the guy behind the knees and making a stumbling fool out of him. No resistance followed as Nolan smashed Vin's head into the wall, twice. The casino employee was holding onto consciousness, his eyes rolled up like a broken slot machine window caught between lemons and cherries. Shoving him bodily down onto the seat, Nolan clutched him by the throat and stared into wide eyes swimming with rage and fear.

"I see you again," Nolan said, "I won't be so forgiving."

Then he slapped the fucker a few hard and fast times and slipped out of the stall. A guy waiting for his turn stopped in mid-step, noticing another guy still seated in there, and Nolan raised a hand.

"Not what you think," he said.

Upstairs, Nolan freshened up, treating himself to his third shower of the day. Then he took a nap till Sherry got back, and when she did, he didn't even mind the packages and sacks that represented a major shopping spree. He was in just too good a mood to care and, anyway, it was her goddamned honeymoon, wasn't it?

She had stopped at the desk and got the key to their new suite.

"We'll drive around to the overflow facility," she said, dangling the key like a single earring. "We can park right outside the suite, motel-style. You have a good time this afternoon?"

"Not bad," he said.

A bellman came up to gather their things, which they'd readied for him, and the couple left the suite and then the casino, retrieving the rental Audi. Sherry had been told the way to the extra building and they drove around behind the main hotel to a three-story square structure with the usual Mardi Gras trim; it frankly looked a little cheap. They exchanged troubled glances.

But when they got into the room, they were pleasantly surprised. Yes, it was tacky, but hey, it was a honeymoon suite, right? Heart-shaped bed, heart-shaped Jacuzzi, pink window curtains, pink shower curtain, pink furniture, Valentine's Day red everywhere else, from carpet to bedspread.

"I think the devil bled to death in here," Nolan said.

"You hopeless romantic," Sherry said, hugging his arm. "I love it. It's so wrong, it's absolutely right…Oh, *flowers*!"

They'd almost missed them, as the dozen roses in a vase on a crimson dresser blended in too well with all that red.

Their things arrived, and Nolan tipped the bellman with the casino's money, and then they tried out the hot tub. Sherry's slender, curvy shape was what hot tubs were designed for, the water making her smooth surfaces slick and shiny; but they knew from past experience that sex was overrated in a Jacuzzi, so the married couple just lounged in the jetting water and washed themselves and each other. Soaping her lovely body, though, including between her legs, inspired him to get on his feet, which in turn prompted her to kneel in the bubbling water and pay him some attention, till they crawled out and finished the session on a spread-out pink towel on the red-carpeted floor nearby.

And it hadn't cost him a dime.

"This married life is okay," he told her from on top of her.

"Isn't it, though?" she said smiling up at him.

They got dressed for their night out—the reservation at Hugo's Cellar was for eight—with Nolan in his milk-chocolate Armani suit and Sherry in a black evening gown with gold fili-gree at the shoulders, a bare back and a side slit. He couldn't wait till he recovered enough to have her again.

Goddamnit, he loved this woman. He'd let himself love a woman once, a long time ago, and then she got herself killed, and he swore off such foolishness. But his life was different now. He wasn't some hard guy thief anymore, was he? He'd tried explaining it to Jon.

Nolan was strictly legit these days, with a beautiful young wife—some might call her a trophy wife…well, the hell with them. He loved her. From the ground up, from the hair down.

Life was good now.

They were just preparing to go out for their evening at one of the best restaurants in Las Vegas, where an old friend and his wife would be waiting, when the men in ski masks and guns burst in.

TWO

8.

Daniel Clifford né Comfort sat at the bar in the restaurant/nightclub called Nolan's in Davenport, Iowa, trying to get the nerve up to ask the bartender a few questions.

The questions wouldn't be hard to ask, but posing them at all bore risks. For example, if after getting rid of Nolan and his live-in girlfriend led to a police investigation—which it surely would—Daniel inquiring about the dead man, before that man got dead, might find its way back to Missouri.

And if Nolan himself returned to this establishment, somebody nosing around about the proprietor of Nolan's might also come back on Daniel. Suppose Nolan entered his house *expecting* someone to be lying in wait.

But what choice did Daniel have?

That note he'd found in Nolan's kitchen indicated a Vegas trip, but no dates were given. He'd checked at the Moline airport and discovered multiple Vegas flights out and back Monday through Sunday, so that was no help.

This was day three for Daniel in Davenport. The first day he'd gone into the home and discovered no one there, but had in the kitchen come across that telltale note that did not tell complete enough a tale. He had gone back in again yesterday, after dark, but not in the early morning hours—around nine, the sun setting maybe half an hour earlier.

Daniel had varied his approach. He again parked the Dart two blocks away, in the opposite direction. He acquired a big grocery bag to put Maw's woven basket in, with the machete stuck in there (lid off to one side to accommodate it), which allowed him to make just one trip from the car to Nolan's house and back again.

Also—and this was key, since he'd be strolling along so much earlier in the evening, with heavier traffic flashing by—Daniel walking with a grocery bag in his arms would look much less suspicious. Either way, though, if a cop found a reason to check him out, he'd have more explaining to do than he might possibly be able to manage. A machete, a lock-picking kit, and a silenced .22 automatic? Explaining the basket wouldn't even come up.

Thanks, Maw.

He had given up on his second night in the house at about the same time he'd broken in the night before. He knew the last possible Vegas flight came in just after eleven P.M. He'd allowed several hours for delays, and for Nolan and the woman to maybe go out for a drink and a meal when they got back. Or perhaps even drive over to his restaurant/club, for Nolan to check back in and see how things had been going while he was away.

So for five hours Daniel had sat in the dark in the finished basement, chain-smoking, waiting for Nolan to enter, hoping Cole's intel about the guy always coming in that way was solid. He entertained the thought that perhaps doing this downstairs would mean he could skip killing the woman, and he fooled himself about that for several hours.

If shooting Nolan in the head and walking away was all, letting the girl keep breathing might have been feasible. But since he had to collect Nolan's head for Maw, that made it impractical to have somebody else running around in the house alive, to interrupt the grisly proceedings or call the cops or even have a gun of her own somewhere to come use on him.

If only Maw wasn't insisting on making a headhunter out of him.

So the next day, Friday, he considered staking the place out and just waiting for Nolan and the woman to come home. But the neighborhood was too upscale for him to risk parking and watching. He made a list at the airport of the various Vegas arrival times, and he bounced from his room at the Starlite to driving past Nolan's place about an hour past each arrival, to see if the travelers were home.

All Daniel did in between was watch TV and smoke and lay on the bed nervous as fucking hell, his stomach churning, his insides roiling. He started crying a few times, not for his potential victims of course, but himself. He called home from the room a few times, but Heather was still pouting. She wouldn't even tell him what she was wearing.

In the early evening, he drove across the I-74 bridge over the Mississippi from Moline to Bettendorf and made his way to Brady Street and drove up the hill to the Brady Eighty shopping center. He parked as near as he could to the restaurant whose neon sign said *Nolan's* in cursive white, but the parking in that part of the big lot was pretty full.

As he got out of the Dart, Daniel wasn't sure whether Nolan's being crowded was good or bad or indifferent. Fearing he'd be too old for this crowd, he'd worn his black suit with two-button jacket and pink shirt with no tie, an ensemble selected for him by Heather at Chess King.

But it proved to be a non-issue. This dark-paneled old-fashioned steakhouse with a smooth jazz combo off in an open side room was not the kind of trendy meat market where he'd met Heather in St. Louis. Oh, it was a meat market all right, but these aged cuts were in their thirties and early forties, a singles crowd he'd guess, mostly divorcés and divorcées, maybe anniversary couples, and he fit right in.

Daniel took a stool at the bar—black padded leather with a

high tufted back, very classy, this Nolan was doing well—and, when the bartender came over, ordered a Snakebite, half cider, half Lager.

He drank it too quickly as he looked around the place, the combo playing "Is It a Crime," the female vocalist doing a nice imitation of Sade, followed by "Smooth Operator." Women with big hair and blue eyeshadow would take a stool up or down from him and it wouldn't take long before a guy would sidle up. Sometimes the guy hit right away, other times not—same for the gals. Last call was a long way off. But seeing couples at tables and in booths, smiling, laughing, flirting, made him miss Heather so much it hurt. Maybe tonight he'd call her and…

"Another?" said the bartender, a shaved-head Latino in his late thirties; he had a black vest with a FRED name tag, a white dress shirt, black bow tie, and muscular look, like maybe he could slide over into bouncer duties if need be.

"Yes, please," Daniel said. "But that's probably my limit, if I want to make it home without a DUI."

The bartender smiled and said, "You got that right. These babies are potent."

When Fred brought the second Snakebite over, and set it down before him, Daniel said, "You make that with a hint of blackcurrant cordial, don't you?"

Fred half-smiled. "We do. Some call it a Snakebite and Black."

"Back home," Daniel said, raising his eyebrows, "we call it a Purple Nasty."

"Where's back home?"

"Minneapolis," Daniel lied. "Say, is the manager around?"

"I'm the assistant manager. Something I can help you with, besides getting you home without a designated driver?"

Daniel gestured vaguely. "I was in here last year—I'm a

salesman with John Deere. Struck up a conversation with the manager. Nolan himself."

"Ah," Fred said noncommittally.

"Turned out we had some mutual acquaintances. Is he around? I don't see him."

"No, he and Sherry—she's the hostess, most nights—are away. On their honeymoon, actually."

Daniel brightened for the guy. "I think I saw her when I was in last year. Beautiful blonde?"

Fred nodded. "Hard to miss her."

"Lucky guy."

The bartender went off to deal with other customers, and ten minutes later he came back to check on Daniel. "Still all right there, my man?"

"Yeah, Fred, this one I'm just nursing. You got any pretzels or anything, to soak this poison up?"

"Sure." Fred went away briefly and came back with a dish of salted peanuts. "Who should I tell the boss was asking for him?"

"Oh, he doesn't know me. We just talked sports and jazz and… I'm in the Cities a few days, though. When do you expect him back?"

"Should be in tomorrow. Gets back around noon."

Fred took care of another customer and Daniel nibbled his peanuts—which, uncomfortably, reminded him of his mother —and finished the Snakebite. He nodded and smiled at Fred on the way out, the combo and their female singer doing "Sweet Love" by Anita Baker.

So Daniel did not spend the night at the ranch-style house in Moline. Instead, after stopping at McDonald's to further soak up those cocktails, he made it back to the Starlite, head still swimming a little. Around ten he called Heather and was relieved to find her home—afraid she was so mad at him she'd go out bar-hopping and God knew what might happen.

She was nice to him on the phone, though. All seemed for-given. After she'd gotten him off by cooing descriptions of what she might or might not have been doing to herself, he fell asleep on the bedspread in a Snakebite-and-Heather induced haze.

Daniel woke up with a hangover that two drinks should not have been able to achieve; but his head was pounding, all right, a real anvil chorus. He drove to a Denny's near the airport where he could fight the condition with high protein—steak and eggs—and that did seem to ease things.

The familiarity of a restaurant that was the same everywhere was somehow soothing. He thought about what he'd learned last night. Sometime this morning, Nolan and Sherry (*that was her name, Fred said, right?*) would fly home, getting in around noon. He had time to get inside that house and be waiting for them when they got back. He could wait downstairs and pop Nolan when the man came in off the patio, and then run up-stairs and take the girl out.

That played out beautifully in his mind several times before reality set in.

The couple was returning from a trip. They would have lug-gage. That meant Nolan's usual entry through the rear entrance was not a sure thing. With suitcases to haul, he might come in through the garage. Or he might leave his car in the drive and he and his new wife would come in the front door with their bags. Alarm keypads were at the ready inside the front door and inside the garage, too, by the door that opened on the kitchen.

And Daniel would be downstairs with his ass hanging out.

Shit.

Better to wait till they were in the sack, asleep, wiped out after their trip. Vegas and honeymoon nookie could take it out of an old guy like this Nolan character. So it would be better to come in at two A.M. again and deal with them in the bedroom, turning their sleep permanent.

That played out in his mind, too, and it was awful.

The girl dead, shot in the head, her brains spattered bloody gray on the headboard, Nolan lying beside her, shot several times non-fatally to make him talk, the bedclothes scarlet with blood, then the shot in the head, more brains, and finally Daniel hauls out the machete and chops Maw a trophy, only things were never that easy in real life, were they? He would have to swing that machete again and again to turn that head into a discon-nected thing, and....

He got up and quickly went into the Denny's can and lost the steak and eggs.

He returned to the booth and had a waitress bring him more coffee.

"Keep it coming," he said, as he sipped the hot bitter liquid.

"You got it, honey."

That scenario, however, the awful horror-show one, was good and goddamn close to what would really occur. He knew that. And he knew, too, that even wounded, Nolan would be the kind of man who wouldn't take dying lying down. He could imagine Nolan waking at the sound of a silenced shot—and silenced shots were not really silenced, not hardly—and finding his new wife dead next to him and leaping at Daniel, managing that even after a bullet tore into and through his leg.

Daniel drank his coffee and sat trembling in his booth, trying not to cry.

Maybe he should just go kill his Maw. She could hardly run from him and would never expect him capable of it. And he knew there was money all over and around that house, stuffed in mattresses, in jars, in boxes, under floorboards, in walls. As long as he timed it when none of her helpers were around, the black girl who cleaned, the handful of accomplices in her fencing business…it would be simple.

The problem was he loved his Maw almost as much as he feared her.

Another possibility was killing Nolan and the girl and *not* taking the man's head. Maybe managing to just kill Nolan and not the girl. Just going to Maw, hat in hand (as opposed to Nolan's head in hands) and saying Nolan was dead all right, but her loving son just couldn't bring himself to cut the corpse's head off. Or maybe something had prevented him from the deed, like a police siren or neighbors pounding at the door or…

Suppose Daniel lied and said he'd killed Nolan after getting a confession that the bastard killed Cole. Maybe that his brother's body had been stuffed in a furnace or woodchipper or something. And that Daniel's only shortfall had been failing to bring back the hated man's head.…

Maw was quite capable, despite all his efforts, of giving him nothing at all. No money, not a nickel, leaving him to face the bank examiners and the music.

This led him to return to the scenario of killing his mother, picturing it vividly in his mind, and then he ran to Denny's john again and puked up two cups of coffee.

Daniel spent the afternoon at the Showcase Cinemas in Milan, also on the Illinois side of the Cities. He went to two movies, sneaking into the second: *Big* with Tom Hanks and *Bull Durham* with Kevin Costner. The first was a comedy, the second a baseball picture. Normally he might have chosen *Rambo III*, but he was in no mood for violence. He had popcorn and a Coke and kept them down.

That was an improvement.

Saturday night—actually Sunday morning—was a repeat of his first night at the ranch-style house in the upscale housing development. He parked a half-a-block down from where he had on his first visit, and again used the shopping bag ruse to save himself a round trip on foot back to the car. He was nervous, but in a keyed-up way. He'd had a catfish and baked potato at Harold's on the Rock and three cups of coffee and cigarette after cigarette, and the food had stayed down, liquid included.

He was ready.

But when, at just after two A.M., he peeked in the windows of the double garage, the woman's 300 ZX was right where it had been the first time. And Nolan's car, a silver Trans Am, Cole's notes said, hadn't been in the driveway and wasn't in the garage next to hers either.

If they'd landed at Moline around noon, as that bartender said, why weren't they home?

Who travels from their honeymoon and then comes home only to go back out and stay away for all hours?

Honeymooners maybe?

No lights were on in the house, not that any of the windows revealed, anyway. For a moment—standing there with a bag of "groceries" in his arms—he almost panicked. Then he decided he had no choice but to go around back and get inside to see what the hell was going on.

Or not going on.

Before picking the lock on the patio door, he set down the grocery bag with the basket and machete, to free up his hands. As he used two picks on the pin tumbler, he knew very well that if no one was home it meant he was picking the lock on a door he himself had locked. The same was true of the keypad when he stepped into the finished basement—he might well be disarming an alarm he had armed himself earlier.

Before sliding the glass door shut behind him, Daniel set the grocery bag inside, then put away his lock picks and got out his silenced .22 and pocket flash. He had repeated this exercise forty-eight hours ago, so he almost knew his way around the pool table and TV area without the flash. But he used it.

As before, he moved carefully, listening, listening, but hearing nothing beyond the ticks of clocks and the hum of appliances. Upstairs, he again made his way down the hall and opened a door he himself had closed to reveal a bed still absent of humans. A made bed, like in the old expression: *you've made your bed, now lie in it.*

So maybe they *were* out partying. People could party later than this. In which case, he should figure out the best place to position himself. But with no sign of suitcases or any other indications large or small that the couple had just returned from a trip (used tickets or magazines or a purse set somewhere) before going back out on the town, Daniel couldn't risk waiting downstairs. The whole process of carting bags inside from a car cast doubt about which way they might enter.

The best thing to do, he decided, was sit in the kitchen. The connecting door to the garage emptied into the kitchen, which was open onto the living room, meaning he could keep an eye on the front door. Whatever door they came through, he'd be waiting with his silenced .22.

He selected a chair from the kitchen table and positioned himself at the best vantage point. He smoked. He waited. He smoked some more. Waited some more. Better than an hour passed.

Having to pee, he got up and went down the hall and used the bathroom. Then his stomach got to him and started roiling, but instead of puking he felt a diarrhea-style attack coming. He sat on the pot and used a Starlite matchbook to light up his latest smoke and shivered there as his body used a different hole for expulsion.

That made Daniel, quite understandably, feel dehydrated, so he got himself another Coors and returned to his chair. Shortly after four in the morning, he fell asleep. When he woke with a start, it scared the hell out of him—waking didn't, but realizing he had let sleep take him in the midst of waiting for a deadly man to return home, a deadly man Daniel was here to kill. Not to mention the deadly man's new bride.

That shook him. The long minutes that followed were hellish, endless things, and at twenty till five—still dark out—he realized Maw would be up by now. He got out of there, going down the stairs and out the back way, setting the alarm first, grabbing up his grocery bag, and walking quickly back to the Dart.

At a 7-Eleven, he bought coffee with a twenty, breaking it to get change for the pay phone back by the restrooms. He dialed his mother's number, feeding coins, and almost hung up, after seven rings, before remembering that she might have to use her walker to get to the phone. He gave it two more rings.

"Mabel speaking," the familiar voice intoned, as if calls this time of morning were common.

"Daniel."

"Daniel ain't here. He don't even live with me."

"Daniel your son! This is your son!"

"…Have you got it?"

"Got what?"

"Information and my prize."

"No. No, neither."

"What the hell you callin' me for then? And what're you callin' me at *all* for? Don't you know there is records of such things. Goodbye!"

"Don't hang up! I'm on a pay phone. This is important."

"Well, talk then."

"Listen close and I'll fill you in." *You old bat,* he added in his mind.

When he was done, she said, "Nothin' mysterious about any of it. He's on his honeymoon. They got to foolin' and fuckin' and extended their trip. That ain't unusual at all. You just keep tryin'."

"What do you mean, keep trying?"

"Sooner or later, they'll come home. You be waitin'. I don't care if it's tomorrow or a week from tomorrow. Got that, dummy?"

"Maw…"

She hung up.

He clutched the receiver and brought it back like a hammer, but then hung it up gently.

At the register, he bought a fresh pack of Kents. He checked for his book of matches, couldn't find it, and took one of the free 7-Eleven ones.

9.

Sherry backed up a step as the gun-wielding figures in black balaclavas, gloves, sweatshirts and jeans rushed into the suite, three of them, the last one hitting the light switch and sending them into darkness. A scream caught in her throat as Nolan, even closer to the door than she was, took a blow to the head with the swing of a gun-in-hand that dropped her husband to the red-carpeted floor. One of the two figures got behind her and a rough-gloved hand came around and covered her mouth and the metal snout of what had to be the automatic in his other hand jammed itself in her lower spine.

Nolan had been knocked to his knees, the assailant slipping behind him to tie her man's hands in back by the wrists with rope, what appeared to be a foot-and-a-half length of clothes-line, knotting it several times, tight. Nolan's head was hanging though his body had not gone slack, so he was dazed but not unconscious.

The third man with a gun was supervising, silhouetted against dim outside lighting. He nodded to the one with his hand over her mouth and the gun in her back, who hauled her outside, into the night and prodded her toward the open rear doors of a black panel truck that was backed up into the stall of the room next door. She saw no one around and the brightly lighted nearby hotel provided the only illumination, as any other exterior lighting back here was, oddly, conveniently, off.

The guy with the hand over her mouth removed it, but the supervisor was there with a strip of duct tape, which he pasted over her mouth. Then her other arm was latched onto and she was lifted and tossed bodily into the panel truck, like a side of beef, and she slid onto the rough indoor-outdoor carpeting on its floor. She landed face down, her black dress up and over the back of her knees. One assailant scrambled up and in and quickly roped her hands behind her and tied her by the ankles as well.

Still on her stomach, her face turned toward the right, staring at a wheel covering in the vehicle's black wall, she heard the thud behind her and knew what it was. Confirming that with a look over her shoulder, she saw Nolan, his mouth duct-taped, too, his eyes open but his apparent grogginess something tough to feign. Some blood was matted on the left side of his head.

A sheet of wood closed off the driver and passenger seat, making a cab out of it, and when the two rear doors—the only visible doors—shut, blackness enveloped them.

She heard the driver's side door open and someone get in and shut it. Then the vehicle rumbled to life; the rider's door opened and someone climbed in and shut it.

"I got everything on this end," said a voice outside the panel truck.

Then they were moving.

She rolled toward Nolan, facing him, or would have been had there been any light at all. They were prone and on their sides with their bound feet near the doors and their heads by the wooden slab that paneled off the driver and rider.

She tried to talk through the duct-tape gag. She said, "Are you all right?" In her ears it sounded like mostly vowels, and she got some vowels back from him, though not as many. The response seemed vaguely positive, at least. She rolled closer, with nothing in mind but being nearer to him. He was on his back, she realized, and she nestled her head on his shoulder and chest and they stayed that way.

The traffic sounds of Vegas faded after maybe ten minutes

and then it got very quiet, just the mechanical hum of the engine and the whir of the tires.

She was going to die.

When the Comforts took her to that cabin, and that hick dope was her captor, she had fought despair and substituted going over her options for escape, her mind sorting through every meager angle on survival, and she'd pursued every one. And she made it through alive, though barely.

She told herself, *And this time Nolan is with me. This time will be different.*

But this time her captors seemed to be driving her, and her husband, not as hostages for ransom, but somewhere to kill them.

And after a while, she thought she knew where.

At least generally, she did. Because sounds besides motor and tire were making themselves heard—the wind rustle of shrubs, the screech of a hawk, the howl of a coyote. They were being taken to die in the desert, weren't they? That vast nowhere surrounding the neon city....

She wept.

Her tears didn't indicate hysteria at all or sorrow, at least not exactly—more something like disappointment. That after everything she and her man had overcome, including the horrors they'd endured six months ago at the whim of those hicks, and the years it took for a relationship of convenience to deepen into something more and for them to find their way to the Little Church...after *all* of that, it would soon be over.

If their captors made it quick, anyway.

Maybe they'd be dumped to die of thirst in the desert, or taken off to be killed slowly over some grudge emanating from Nolan's past, the seemingly endless supply of bad karma he'd managed to accumulate.

When her tears subsided, he asked her something through

his own duct-taped gag; it might have been what she'd asked him earlier: "Are you okay?"

At least "hmmm hmmm" was easy to get across through a wedge of tape. She wondered if her quiet crying had somehow been apparent to him, the gentle heaving of her body, perhaps a moaning she hadn't realized she'd made.

Would he think less of her for that?

Finally the vehicle slowed and a trembling of anticipation— *has dying time come?* —overtook her. She sensed no similar physical reaction from the man whose chest she leaned against.

They stopped with a shudder, as if even the panel truck had qualms.

The doors opened and two men—apparently two of the three in black balaclavas who had burst into the suite—hauled them out, one taking her, the other Nolan. Both man and wife were able to get onto their feet and stay upright.

The night was dark and a toenail clipping of moon didn't do much to relieve it, though some ivory was cast on their surroundings—an ancient roadside motel, blistered pink with green trim, a single row of eight rooms with an office in the middle, a modest swimming pool off to one side full of leaves and refuse and no water, all overseen by a weathered sign, its neon not glowing and perhaps long burnt-out, that had

MUSHROOM
MOTEL

superimposed over a cartoon cloud of an atomic blast.

Only two cars were in the stalls out front—a late model Chevy pick-up in front of the office (a sign said CLOSED), and an old but well-maintained white-trimmed red Thunderbird in the next stall over.

Nolan was alert now and taking it all in.

The night was cool, she noticed. Almost cold. She'd always heard it could get chilly at night in the desert, and now she knew it was true.

"Welcome, folks," a casual, midrange male voice said.

She glanced over where a medium-size man in his sixties had come out of the office. He ambled over, sneakers stirring parking lot gravel, hands in the pockets of baggy tan slacks, a yellow sweater loose over a white Ban-Lon sports shirt, all draped over a skinny frame. He had a gray-white butch haircut, teeth big and cigarette-stained in a friendly face that split the difference between handsome and goofy.

The two men hauling them paid their apparent host little heed. He strolled over and said affably, "Can't pretend you've chosen our little home away from home of your own volition… but that doesn't mean the missus and me won't do our best to make your stay no more unpleasant than need be."

Sherry and Nolan were listening to this while two of the masked men were holding onto them with a gun in the back and a choking arm around the neck.

"You're in number six," their host said, walking out ahead, pointing.

Sherry and Nolan were dragged to the door marked 6 and their host opened it and reached in around to switch on the light.

Their captors were gentlemen, apparently—Sherry was ushered in first, and then Nolan.

The overhead light was weak and yellow. The room held a bare ancient mattress with piss stains and random springs seeking escape. The plaster walls were pink and cracked, the furniture limited to a single dresser dating to the 1950s with its mirror gone, just the framing remaining. The floor was pink-and-black linoleum, faded and scarred and curling at the edges. A bathroom had no door, the lack of which revealed a pot with no lid. The room had a musty smell partially cut by air freshener. Thoughtful.

The most notable feature was a hole in the wall next to the dresser and opposite the bed, essentially a ragged doorway into the adjacent room where a TV was going, like maybe a sledgehammer made it. *Perfect Strangers* was on.

Their two burly black-masked escorts tossed their charges on the bed with a metallic *whump* of springs raising some dust, then nodded to their host in the doorway. He entered and they went out. Then the panel truck was spitting gravel as it pulled out of the parking lot and headed off into the night.

"My name is Ozzie," their host said, gesturing to himself and offering up a ridiculous smile.

His skin had a gray look but his blue eyes had sparkle. He was standing by the dresser, facing the two guests on their backs on the filthy mattress with tape on their mouths and their hands roped behind them and ankles tied, Nolan's Armani suit rumpled, her black dress up over her bare legs, torn and disarrayed, her high-heel shoes M.I.A.

"You'll meet Harriet, my better half, shortly." A grin blossomed. "Not our real names, as you might have guessed."

Sherry and Nolan exchanged sideways glances over their duct-tape gags.

"Let's start with this," Ozzie said, and he drew back his sweater to put his hand on his hip. Doing so, he exposed the big automatic pistol stuffed in his waistband.

"Harriet and I consider you to be our guests. But the freight is paid by our Vegas friends, so their word is law. We don't know why you're here, except it's because you displeased them in some way. We don't know how long you'll be staying. So please don't trouble yourselves, or us, by bothering us about it."

Ozzie began to pace slowly, gesturing, not looking at them as he said, "Some of our guests are here a short while—our Vegas friends question them about this and that, not our concern. Some of you they send back home while the other stays here, and I assume money to repay a debt is bein' put together. Again, not our role. Not our business."

Ozzie paused to light up a cigarette. A Chesterfield from a pack in his sweater pocket.

He waved out a match and puffed some gray smoke about the color of his complexion, then said, "Some of you stay a night or two and then go on about your way, in the company of those who paid for your stay. Where you wind up is between you and them and we have nothin' to do with it."

His pacing stopped and he was facing the door and seemed to be looking through it, to the world beyond. Now and then he would take a drag and hold it deep, then let out a cloud of gray.

"I will tell you frankly, as you look like a nice couple, and someone let it slip you were recently wed…congratulations. Best of luck, really. It's a wonderful institution, marriage…but who wants to live in an institution?"

He laughed and pawed the air with his cigarette in hand and said, "Forgive an old married man his little joke."

His expression grew more serious as he looked right at them now. "I only wish this was a few years ago and you were stayin' with us in our heyday. Clear up to twenty years ago, we had couples from all over these United States stay with us. Crew from a John Wayne movie did, too, shooting out in the desert. We were a destination!"

He looked at the ceiling, maybe seeing the sky on the other side. "Back in '52, when the little woman and me first opened up, those mushroom clouds at the test site wasn't just lightin' up the sky, but our cash register too! Oh, we had competition, all right—Binion's and the Desert Inn, facin' north like that, could have their A-bomb parties at dawn and peddle their atomic cocktails. But *we* had the first Miss Atomic Energy contest, *not* the Sands. And they was sixty-five miles away, and we were only thirty! Hell of a view from here! Sight to see."

Suddenly the friendly face clenched into an ugly fist. "Then they go and stop testing aboveground after that Cuban missile deal, and, poof, the party was over."

He swung to face them and shook a finger at Sherry and Nolan, as if all of this had been their fault.

"If it wasn't for our Vegas friends," he said, spittle flying, "this place would have been out of business a long time ago! I mean, they been our only customers since '65."

A frail-looking woman in a blue-and-white A-line dress came in the door with a tray of Coca-Cola, five sweating eight-ounce bottles, as if she were a hostess serving Sherry and Nolan on the back porch. A small revolver was also on the tray, which she set on the dresser.

Their hostess was small and not just skinny, like Ozzie, but nearly skeletal, and even grayer. Very pretty, though, even if that much makeup gave her a *What Ever Happened to Baby Jane* look.

"Ozzie! Is this any way to treat our new guests?"

He turned to her and looked a little embarrassed with himself. "Honey, I'm afraid I got to yammering and just didn't tend to business. I'm sorry, dear." He took one of the Cokes and had a swig, gulping it down. "I should have made these folks more comfortable, before goin' on and on about this and that."

"You'll have to forgive my husband," she said to her bound and gagged guests, her smile sweet, her teeth as gray as the rest of her. "He's a talker."

"This is Harriet," he said to them, with a *pre-senting* gesture. "But I guess you guessed that….*Lou! Bud!*"

A stirring in the room through the hole in the wall produced a short chubby mustached man, who walked through without ducking, and a taller guy with stringy long hair, who did have to duck. They looked nothing alike except for the dead eyes. Fortyish, they wore matching light blue track suits and running shoes, each with a shoulder-holstered pistol, brown leather with cotton elastic harness. It was not a good look.

"The gentleman first," Harriet said, nodding toward the mattress and the man on it.

With no further instruction, the pair went to Nolan, turned him face down roughly and the fat little man began untying the rope while the taller guy put the nose of his automatic at the back of Nolan's skull. The chubby guy apparently had done this before, because the nasty knots came deftly undone at his touch.

When the length of clothesline was loose, the chubby one turned Nolan back over, like he was frying both sides of a sausage, and the skinny one put the nose of his gun in Nolan's neck while the chubby one retied Nolan's hands in front.

Then the process was repeated with Sherry, but with a gentler touch and without pressing the nose of the gun to her flesh, though it had been plenty close enough.

"Thank you, Lou," Harriet said, nodding to the chubby one, "thank you, Bud," nodding to the skinny one.

Grinning, Ozzie said, "Not *their* real names, neither."

The skeletal woman made a whirling gesture with a finger. "You can sit, you two. Sit up."

They did, the mattress creaking and groaning, as if it were the real victim here.

"Go ahead," Ozzie said, "and take that tape off your mouths."

Nolan fingered off the sticky strip and Sherry did, too.

Harriet gave them each a Coke, which they accepted with their limited range of motion, thanks to locked wrists.

Sherry drank some of the icy liquid. She had never tasted anything better. Seemed things really did go better.

Nolan had a swig, too. His eyes were fixed on them like a cobra's on a lesser snake.

"You have a working toilet here," Harriet said matter-of-fact, and nodded toward the doorless bathroom. "You can hop in there and use it as you like. Depending on how long you're with us, you may have a snack or a meal brought to you now and then."

Bud and Lou were standing at either side of Harriet and Ozzie now, their arms folded like bored eunuchs outside a harem door.

"When we leave," Ozzie said, "feel free to converse, but keep the noise down. The boys don't like to be disturbed while they watch their shows."

Bud and Lou affirmed that with nods.

"You need something," Harriet said, "call out. Lou or Bud will…"

But the frail woman began to cough. It was a terrible racking thing, and Ozzie slipped an arm around her shoulders. "You'll be fine, honey. You'll be fine, darling girl."

She stopped coughing, then resumed. "Lou or Bud will check on you, and summon us if there's a need. But your world here is not large. This mattress, that toilet. Stay in this world or answer the consequences. Understood?"

Nolan nodded slowly.

Seeing that, Sherry nodded, too.

Bud and Lou looked at Ozzie and Harriet to see if any other instructions were forthcoming, and when they weren't, they each took a Coke from Harriet's tray, and then the duo slipped through the ragged hole in the wall into their quarters.

Gathering the now empty tray, Harriet coughed again, not as long but just as deep, then went to the door and stood there, waiting as her husband opened it for her.

Harriet did not look at their guests again, but Ozzie paused to say, "We'll check on you in the morning. Bring you some juice and sweet rolls."

He smiled and nodded and waved a little, hitting the light switch as he went out.

They were in darkness.

Miami Vice was on in the adjacent room.

They spoke in whispers, and with the TV loud enough in the next room for them to do so with little risk.

"I think Harriet," Nolan said, "got a little too close to those atomic blasts. And I bet they never had a David or Ricky."

"Her husband is crazy."

"Not so crazy that he didn't let us know he's armed. This is a Bonnie and Clyde motel with Bonnie and Clyde running it."

"What do we do?"

"We wait to see if Abbott and Costello are our permanent guards or if there's another shift. If they're the whole party, then we might be able to pull something after everybody's asleep."

"Who did this to us?"

"Somebody with the French Quarter."

"You sound sure of that."

"One of the guys that grabbed me tonight was Vin—his mask's eye holes gave him away—white eyebrows."

"Who is Vin?"

"One of the pair that hauled me off this morning when they thought I was casing the casino. He got a little rougher than need be, so I caught up with him later and paid him back some."

Karma didn't quit, did it?

She said, "*He's* behind this?"

"No. He's a cog. What I want to know is…why are we still alive?"

"Any ideas?"

"Maybe they intend to keep you, and let me go rustle up a ransom. Judging by what our chatty friend Ozzie said, that's what this place is used for, among other things."

"What other things?"

"Probably beat the shit out of cheaters, particularly teams using signals and the like. Pound on losers and send them home to pay up, kind of thing."

"Not kill them?"

"That's not what this place is for. It's for scaring the shit out of people and beating the shit out of them, yes. But not for killing them. I don't think Ozzie and Harriet signed on for that. Besides, who needs to put somebody up at a shithole like this for a few fun days and then take them out to the desert and fill a hole?"

"Nolan…please…"

"Sorry. Anyway, you don't need an appointment in the desert —it's open 24/7. We'd be dead already if that's what this is about…I think."

"You think?"

"There's maybe a reason otherwise, but…"

"What?"

"Maybe somebody wants us…*me*…dead, but doesn't want that till the timing is right."

"That doesn't make sense."

"Forget it. Bigger fish to fry right now.…Here." He lifted his bound arms and had her slip under them so they could be closer together. Hug without hugging. He kissed her. A really long, slow tender kiss that she would never forget.

Of course, she might not have much time to remember it.

Their faces close, noses almost touching, she said, "Who would do something like this to us? To you?"

"Oh, I know who did this," he said.

10.

The hardest part about stealing the skim, Harry Bellows knew, was not getting killed.

Making the monthly run itself wasn't hard at all—three hours and maybe fifteen minutes (without stops) up Highway 95 to the small private airport outside Tonopah where he would hand off the bag of money to the regular courier for transport to Chicago, or more specifically to the Rouse House, a suburban illegal casino of the Outfit's. Tonopah was about halfway between Reno and Vegas and was a convenient shipping point for skim for both casino cities.

The skim, though it went to Chicago, was distributed between there and Cleveland, Kansas City, and Milwaukee, who all had silent interests in the French Quarter. This practice extended back to Bugsy Siegel's skimming his take to pay back mob investors in cash and avoid IRS attention. The casino's monthly skim rarely ran less than $500,000 and business of late had been especially good. This month the skim, Harry knew, could approach $700,000.

For three years now, he'd been one of the rarefied few allowed into the counting room to fill a briefcase with the allotted cash to make the monthly drive to a waiting courier at the little Tonopah airport, in the company of his regular bodyguard, Vin, who'd had the assignment over a year. He and Vin had become friendly over that time, and Harry even shared with Vin his fantasy about taking just one skim run for himself, to retire on. It had been a joke that evolved into a running gag into a half-serious notion and finally into a plan.

Harry considered himself an honest man and had never lifted a nickel from his employers; but at fifty-eight well-fed years of age, he was someone who had never worked for anybody but the Chicago Outfit. Which meant he was well aware that crime paid his bills and kept a roof over his head. Harry Bellows had been in the employ of organized crime from his first Rush Street job on, fronting assorted legal activities of theirs, along the way witnessing, and enabling, illegal acts from money-laundering to murder cover-ups.

Five years ago when the French Quarter opened, Harry had been there from day one, in a job that had initially seemed a step up, and a yearly salary of $50,000 that seemed fair enough. But his raises had been minimal, bonuses nonexistent, and, with a retirement not many years away, he had come to realize "Executive Host" was the last rung on his ladder, the last, dead-end stop of his career.

In a way Harry had been his own worst enemy. He knew that. He was just too damn good with people—his affability, his likeability, condemned him to roam the casino rather than inhabit the twentieth floor where the real executives had offices that weren't cubbyholes off the kitchen. His pension package wasn't bad, but it wasn't good, either. And his age was against him. The Quarter had a habit of putting you out to pasture when you got much past sixty.

Maybe if he wasn't so heavy, Harry thought, he might feel confident of hanging on longer at the casino; but his weight had always been a problem. Since childhood, he'd been a nervous eater, and everybody in his family had been large. He'd done what he could to compensate, learning to be a classic hail-fellow-well-met. He'd always made sure to dress well, and though he was told he had a face like Rock Hudson, his body was more William Conrad.

He'd started dyeing his hair, but that didn't help, and girdles were painful. He expressed opinions and ideas to the execs, and had kissed up to the new top manager, this Briggs golden boy, twenty years younger than Harry and half as experienced. None of that brought any sign of interest in anything he had to say from Briggs or the rest of the top-floor crowd. Flattery about how well he was doing in his host position was the best he ever got.

Six months ago, his wife Stella moved out of their ranch-style in Charleston Heights. Their son, Chris, was still in town, studying business at UNLV, sharing an apartment with his girl-friend. Stella's method of dealing with empty nest syndrome had been to empty the nest further—she and two divorced gals were sharing a condo now, and she was dating around.

Harry and Stella had never really argued. She had looked up to him once, when he was a real executive at the Four Queens and she a lowly cocktail waitress...but a beautiful one, a voluptuous redhead. As the years went by, however, she grew increasingly bored with him. Even so, she'd been a dutiful mother to Chris, a good homemaker, and didn't run around on him that he knew of. It was just that she was kind of a...complainer.

His inability to rise through the ranks at the Quarter made it obvious she'd thought she was hitching her wagon to a star, not a blimp. They still had sex, but not often, and because of his weight, the positions they employed were limited. Missionary style had been out for some time.

And she was always talking about wanting a nicer house. When they moved in five years ago, their subdivision—while hardly one of the newest or most desirable in Vegas—had seemed fine to her. They had three bedrooms, three baths, a big family room and a fireplace.

But the little brown ranch-style with the modest yard appeared only to depress her now—the appliances that had come with the place were badly out of date. They didn't have a swimming pool, like many other couples they knew, and not a big enough back yard to put one in. She was limited in what food she could buy, what kind of clothes she could afford, or new furniture, never having anything really nice....

He wished he didn't still love her.

It didn't help that she was still a knockout, well into her forties. The tits were big and high and firm, her ass round and tight; she had a little tummy, but who was he to talk? And when she had a glass of wine or two, she was sweet and funny and tender. That was when they would make love. Wine seemed to ease the whining.

So now he was sitting opposite her in Hugo's Cellar at the Four Queens, the casino/hotel in Glitter Gulch where they had both once worked, when he had romanced her and she had thought he was going places. Well, he had. Just not in the right direction.

"You look fantastic," he said to her, and she did, in a black bare-shouldered cocktail dress with a cut that showed off her full bosom.

They were drinking wine, Blue Nun, her favorite. He thought it tasted a little like fingernail polish remover, or what he imagined that would taste like. But whatever Stella liked, he wanted to give her. He just hadn't always been able to afford to.

"Thanks," she said. Her wide, full lips twitched him a smile, her dark blue eyes hooded with lighter blue on the lids. She had a pretty, heart-shaped face with a pug nose.

Stella had once worked in this red-brick, intimate restaurant, where the tips were very good—Harry, in fact, had seen to it that she got a position here, the choicest spot at the Queens for a cocktail waitress.

Tonight he'd encouraged her to order anything she'd like. She'd gone for Dover Sole, he the Beef Wellington. With the wine and dessert, he would spend well over one hundred bucks. She would, he knew, like that. It would sit her up and make her pay attention.

Which was why she was studying him now.

"Harry," she said, after a sip of Blue Nun, "this isn't going to work."

"What isn't?"

Half a smile was bequeathed to him. "One nice night out doesn't get me back."

He gave her an easy grin. "The question is, gorgeous, what *does* get you back?"

The bare shoulders shrugged. "I'm not sure...anything."

Their food came and they ate in polite silence; occasionally he would smile at her, with a twinkle in his eyes (he hoped), and she would smile back, if grudgingly, though several times her eyes tightened, her expression saying, *What is he up to?*

When their dishes had been cleared, Harry ordered Cherries Jubilee, a specialty here, served tableside—her favorite. She watched mesmerized as the flaming dish was prepared, then ate her serving slowly, her expression as close to orgasmic as he'd seen on that pretty face in ages. He watched her closely as she finished, since he'd put away his serving before she was barely beginning.

Harry had coffee and she continued with wine, as he said, "Where would you live, sweetheart, if you could live anywhere?"

The pretty face made itself ugly. "*Not* Vegas. You *know* I hate this town. The tourists are a pain in the butt and the locals are burnouts from this place and that, and the only thing those two groups have in common is being horrible drivers. And the goddamn *heat*. Fuck this shit, anyway."

"Not Vegas. Kind of knew your feelings on that score, gorgeous. So. Where?"

Her shrug was quick this time. "Do I have to tell you? Back in Duluth, of course, where my folks are, and my brothers and sisters."

Where she'd been the queen of the prom and the head cheerleader and riding high till she flunked out of the university and went to Vegas to be a showgirl. And wound up at the Four Queens…and she was back, wasn't she?

"Housing is reasonable up there," he said. "Compared to here, anyway."

"I suppose it is. Why would you know that?"

He gave her a sly smile; it was calculated, like so many looks he had ever given her in their marriage. "Because I've looked into it. We could sell our house in Charleston Heights and move into something better up there and still come out ahead."

She made another face. "*You* leave *here?* What, and work in an Indian casino, maybe? You couldn't pass the physical."

He shook his head. "Not work in a casino. Retire."

That rated a laugh. "Are you kidding? You'll never retire, Harry."

"Oh yes I will." He reached over and touched her hand. "If you could put up with life here with me for another five years, I'd take early retirement, and we could move you back home."

She looked at his hand on hers but didn't do anything about it. "Five years here is an eternity."

He withdrew his hand before she could hers. "Well…in a year or two, I could probably get away with saying I'm having health problems. Con the twentieth-floor crowd into letting me retire even earlier."

Her smirk was skeptical. "What would *that* do to your pension? Which is already shitty, I might add."

"I think they'd give me full pension. And it *is* shitty, but better than nothing."

She had another sip of Blue Nun. She always said she liked it because you could drink it all the way through dinner and beyond.

"Harry, you're a sweet guy," she said patronizingly. "I never said you weren't. The nicest guy I was ever with, even if that isn't saying much. But if I didn't like life in Vegas on fifty grand a year, what makes you think I want to live in Minnesota on a fraction?"

"May I ask you something, darling?"

She raised her glass to him, said archly, "Oh by all means," and had another sip.

He cocked his head and trotted out the sly look again. "What would you say if I told you I had an opportunity to make a lot of money?"

"I would say you are full of shit, Harry."

He held up a palm. "No. Really. But it…wouldn't be strictly legal. Well…not legal at all."

He had her attention now. Really had it. The dark blues managed to focus on him.

Stella leaned in. "I would not give a diddly damn if your 'opportunity' were as crooked as a dog's hind leg, lover boy. Who do you think you've been working for all these years?" She whispered: "The goddamn Mafia, in case you never noticed."

"You're right, dear. And when you're right, you're right."

"How much?"

"Money am I talking?"

"No, how much money are you spending on me tonight to try to get my sweet ass in bed tonight? We haven't been to Hugo's since three anniversaries ago."

He raised both palms now, in surrender. "I am not trying to get your sweet ass in bed tonight."

"I don't believe you."

"Approximately seven hundred thousand dollars. Tax free."

Her big blue eyes got very big, white all around, and her red-lipsticked mouth got round, too. She wasn't as pretty with that expression on her face, yet he couldn't help thinking about how much he'd like to slide his stiff prick in there, just the same.

"We'd be living on my pension and our savings," he said, very quietly, "as far as anyone would know. We'll have a lovely house, we'll travel as much as we please, *eat* as well as we please, a cleaning woman will come in once a week, no, *twice* a week, you'll buy any and all the clothes you like, a health club if you like, belong to the country club…the whole megillah."

She was smiling just a little, and trying very hard to make herself sober. "Who do you have to kill?"

Vin, for one. And a few others.

"No one," he said casually. He took her hand again and squeezed. "It's just money waiting to be taken, darling. Very low risk. You don't need to know any more than that."

"I don't *want* to know any more than that."

They stopped at her apartment and got her things, and she moved back in. When he fucked her, he climbed on top and she seemed to like it just fine.

The next morning, an hour before he and Vin were due to pick up the skim, Harry walked the casino floor, nodding and smiling, a bundle of conflicting thoughts and emotions free-falling through him.

Overjoyed as he was having Stella back, the price would include killing Vin, who was after all something of a friend, and a part of Harry's life right now. Killing Nolan, who was not in Harry's current life, represented a loss less keenly felt. Anyway, he and Nolan had never been *that* close, and that young piece of tail from the Tropical, Sherry? She was just a little fucking gold digger.

Nolan calling Harry to help make honeymoon arrangements —when would an opportunity like that come along again? A notorious thief, well-known to the Quarter's Chicago connections, walks into Harry's hopes and dreams, making them come true by unintentionally offering to take the blame! That had always been the missing element in Harry and Vin's scheme— no one to play the patsy. Who was it said, *I love it when a plan comes together?*

Harry had, of course, been the one to point Nolan out on the security-cam monitors in the Eye in the Sky, with Vin primed to be on the lookout for Nolan in the casino. That black guy that Vin worked with, Leo, hadn't been aware a sort of fix was in.

Vin had gone all in, ready to bring to life the scheme they'd daydreamed over the past year—specifically, the nondescript Ford Taurus used on the Tonopah run would be found on the roadside on Highway 95 with both Harry and Vin on the ground beside the car, pistol-whipped, their briefcase of money (supposedly) taken.

Not that the plan wasn't without risk or for that matter physical pain. First, Vin would have to slap Harry with his nine millimeter alongside the head, get some blood and bruising going, and then Harry was to do the same with Vin...only instead of hitting him similarly, Harry would put a bullet in his accomplice's brain.

Harry supposed there was a chance that Vin might try a double-cross himself; but he doubted Vin had the balls or the necessary deficit of brains needed to just snatch the casino money and run off and try to disappear into a world that had so many mob guys in it.

No, they both had to be found by the car with the money missing. That would be the second part of putting the plan into play. First they would stop at the Mushroom Motel and, well, what followed would be as unpleasant as it was necessary....

The two gun thugs, "Bud" and "Lou"—standing guard on Nolan and his new wife—were low-level, off-the-books casino employees who collected debts locally and who did watchdog duty at the Mushroom when somebody was getting a beating. Now and then somebody was being held till somebody else paid off. Occasionally, a "guest" checked in at the Mushroom to receive room-service torture until giving up information of one kind or another, and then were checked out and escorted into the desert for a nature walk.

Getting rid of those two knotheads would hardly change the course of Western Civilization, much less lose Harry any sleep.

He did feel bad about Ozzie and Harriet, but they would be (as they said in espionage circles) collateral damage. The couple would be a loss to the casino, and possibly the motel would have to be shut down, its special function moved elsewhere, since the killings might be tough to cover up; but what did he care? Hell, Harry was surprised Ozzie and Harriet were both still alive, after all the radiation they'd been exposed to.

The scenario was complicated, but he'd played it out in his mind so many times, it now seemed straightforward and even simple.

Harry and Vin would enter the room where Nolan and the girl were being held. Harry would hold a finger to his lips to shush Nolan and the girl, and would indicate by gesture that he was there to rescue them. Then Harry would call out to Bud and Lou. When Bud and Lou came through the hole in the wall, to see what was up, Vin would shoot them both in the head. Then when Ozzie and Harriet came in, in response to the gunshots—most likely through the door to Nolan's room—then Vin would shoot them, too.

By agreement, Vin would hand the gun to Harry, who would shoot the couple on the bed.

Murdering the two women didn't really bother Harry. Harriet was a nasty old piece of work, and Sherry was a user. But, as his brain continued to remind him, Nolan had been a friend of sorts. Harry wished he could leave that unhappy task to Vin, but it seemed like leaving all the killing to Vin was wrong.

Of course Harry was not fool enough to think you could plan something like that to the letter. Getting rid of six people, in a few minutes, or even seconds—two by his own hand! The possibility of fucking up or encountering the unexpected was undeniable.

But the rewards were substantial—money and Stella and happy Golden Years. He was thinking this as he smiled at an older couple who were heading to the slots with plastic buckets of quarters. They smiled back and waved. He'd welcomed them when they checked in.

Harry felt confident that the aftermath would play out as he envisioned it. When the casino guys got to the Mushroom, they would find—in a scene staged by Harry—Nolan and the others shot to death with an empty briefcase left behind, suggesting a third thief in the scheme had betrayed his accomplices and booked it with the money in some other means of transport. Forensics would find the same gun doing all the killing, which indicated a missing guilty party.

Nolan and Sherry were being kept alive at the moment because Harry knew that if they'd been killed earlier, their times of death would not gibe with the discovery of the Taurus (and dead Vin). No, Nolan and the girl needed to be freshly killed when Harry was found unconscious with his dead bodyguard Vin near a car with no briefcase of money in the back.

"Hey!" a midrange, youthful voice called out over the casino noise. "Mr. Bellows!"

Harry stopped and turned, as Nolan's friend Jon came jogging up. He was in a Blondie t-shirt and jeans and sneakers and looked about eighteen, though if that were the case he wouldn't be allowed in here.

"Listen," Jon said, out of breath, "I'm a little worried."

"Whatever for?"

He gestured vaguely. "I was supposed to meet Nolan and Sherry for breakfast at seven. It's almost eight now and no sign of them."

"Seven's a little early, is it?" Harry said with a smile he almost meant.

"For normal people. But Nolan's an early riser, in his old age, and he and Sherry have a big day planned. Lake Mead stuff this morning, golf for him this afternoon and sunning for her, then tickets to the Everly Brothers tonight..."

Harry put a hand on Jon's shoulder. "Okay, son. But it's not even eight o'clock yet."

Jon shook his head. "Nolan is never late."

He smiled reassuringly. "Maybe, but he's a married man now, and on his honeymoon, so...?"

"I knocked on that new suite of theirs. Nothing. Listen, Mr. Bellows—I know you and Nolan go way back. So you know I'm not just being paranoid, wanting to check and make sure he's okay. Especially after what happened yesterday morning."

Harry looked serious, nodding. "No, I do understand."

Another vague gesture. "So can you fix me up with somebody who can check out their room? See if they're okay? I'm probably overreacting, but—"

"No. Not overreacting at all." Harry had just had a thought. "I'll go over with you myself. I have a passkey. We'll walk there through the casino, but give me a moment..."

The executive host stepped away, putting some crowd between him and Jon, and he spoke a few words into his walkie.

In under five minutes, they were at Nolan's suite on the ground floor of the overflow facility. Harry used his passkey and then stepped inside, Jon following and then edging past.

Everything looked fine in the room of garish reds. No sign, Harry noted with pleasure, of the struggle last night. Jon poked around at this and that, obviously not quite knowing what he was looking for, and didn't notice at first when Vin stepped in the open door. Jon didn't start to turn till Vin was almost on top of him, swinging the automatic with its butt facing out.

Jon went down in a pile and lay motionless on the pink carpet, blood in his blond hair going well with the room.

Harry checked outside—nobody around.

"Move it," he said to Vin, who already had Jon under the arms, dragging him.

Together they tossed him in the trunk of the waiting backed-up Taurus and quickly Harry used duct tape on Jon's slack wrists and ankles, then covered his mouth with a silver strip. The kid was still out. Probably not dead.

Vin shut the trunk.

Harry grinned at Vin. "I think we found the third man."

"What third man?"

"The missing accomplice in a robbery that hasn't quite happened yet."

11.

Nolan allowed himself to sleep. Sherry lay close, after sliding up and under his bound hands, which were now at the small of her back. She was pressed against him now, deep asleep, purring more than snoring.

He counted on the circumstances keeping him in a light slumber only, as he wanted to be awake by three A.M. or so. They'd snatched off his wristwatch at some point, when he was half-unconscious, but he'd always had a good inner clock. When he woke to darkness with only the very occasional sound of a car going by on Highway 95, he roused Sherry with a gentle shake, confident the timing was right.

She came awake at once, and he said, "Shhhh." She swallowed, looked a bit disoriented, then got her bearings.

He whispered, "Slip out and under," meaning the embrace of his arms and roped hands.

She did so, but still stayed close.

They spoke only in the most barely audible whispers.

"I had to wait," he said, "till I could assume they were asleep."

She nodded. Bud and Lou had apparently nodded off with the TV going, because through the hole in the wall they could see the little set on a stand, its picture snowy and the sound hissing. The latter was loud enough to give their conversation some cover. The former aided their night vision, as did moonlight filtering in the curtained windows onto the road.

"It's about four," Nolan said. "Hour and a half till sunrise."

She nodded.

"There's a bed spring next to me," he said. He pointed and

she sat up and saw the spring seeking escape from the grimy mattress.

Nolan went on: "I'm going to use it to work at these." He raised his bound wrists, lowered them. "Won't go fast."

She nodded.

"If I really go at it," he said, "this mattress will get noisy. So be patient."

"Not going anywhere."

He nodded. Smiled. "Keep your eyes on that hole in the wall. I'll be on my side with my back to you. Working this. Nudge me if one of them's coming."

She nodded. Then she kissed him. It lasted a while.

"We've had better times," he said, "in motel rooms."

She grinned. It was desperate, but it was a grin.

And he began working at the ropes. It was one rope, really, looped three times around his wrists, which meant cutting through all three. The sprung spring had a sharp end, so it went a little faster than he'd figured, but he couldn't put a lot of energy into it, or (as he'd said to Sherry) the fucking mattress might betray him.

The rope was plaited braid, four different sets of strands woven and intertwined. Square braid, as it was called, tended to feel coarse, easy to knot but also easily damaged. That was a real break.

It took him half an hour to get through that first loop.

He told her, "Progress."

She swallowed and nodded.

The mattress *did* squeak as he worked, but not enough to rise above the white noise of the TV next door. The world beyond the curtained window was brightening, sun threatening to come up. He kept at it. And at it.

Finally the second loop gave.

He tried to see if the third loop, which was a little looser than the other two, might be snugged up over his wrists and hands. He couldn't get at it well enough with his fingers, so rolled toward Sherry and enlisted her help. She got the loop to just below his wrist bone, the plaited rope displaying some limited flexibility, stopping where his thumb jutted, getting no further.

He returned to working the spring at the remaining rope.

When it finally gave, he grinned at her and she beamed at him. Quickly he untied her wrists, then got his ankles untied, while she got her own ankles free. Thick though the knotting was, loosening it was not difficult.

Nolan slipped off the mattress. He was in his stocking feet, his shoes having been confiscated before he was stuffed in that panel truck. He cautioned Sherry with a hand—she was sitting up but staying put.

Moving slow and quiet, he went to the motel room door. He turned the knob, wincing as he did; it made just a little noise before letting him know the goddamn thing was locked. He crept to the window past Sherry's side of the mattress. He tugged back half of the drawn curtain and metal bars greeted him.

Well, shit.

He returned to the mattress and climbed back on it next to her. He whispered, "I could use a gun."

"Fresh out."

He thought about their situation. His alternatives for make-shift weaponry were limited—a drawer from the dresser to break over a head, or maybe the tank lid of the toilet, to batter somebody? Best bet were the two small empty Coke bottles, which were heavy glass. But, Jesus....

Still whispering, he said, "Options. I go through that hole in the wall and take my chances with those sleeping dopes. Maybe with a Coke bottle club. Might be a gun to grab before they stir."

"Or?"

He shrugged. "Play possum. Wait for them to check us."

"Yeah. That."

"Agreed. Now, they'll likely check me first. When one gets close to me, you roll off your side of the bed because I'll be grabbing the bastard."

"Let me tackle the other one."

"No. Bullets may be flying. My job is to get one of their guns. Yours is to keep your head down."

"Nolan…"

"Love, honor and obey, remember? This is the obey part."

Nolan looped rope around his ankles and did the same with his wrists, and positioned himself so it appeared he was still bound, with the knots just not showing. Sherry followed suit. Then they began feigning sleep.

Through the hole in the wall, Nolan and Sherry could see Bud, still in the light blue-and-white track suit, pass through their line of vision on his way somewhere to the right. Soon the drumming of a shower could be heard. Then Lou, also still in his track suit, wandered into view to turn the channel onto the NBC morning news. The shower stopped and, before long, an electric shaver announced itself, and after a couple minutes, a toilet flushed, followed by some water running in the sink.

Bud wandered into view, his bathroom duties attended to— but back in that same track suit—and Lou took his turn showering, shaving, shitting and so on. The network news became local. Lou returned also wearing his track suit.

Bud and Lou, freshly bathed if in yesterday's clothes, stepped inside Room #6 through their hole in the wall, and from that vantage took a look at Nolan and Sherry, apparently asleep on the mattress and bound as before, and ducked back into their quarters.

"Fuck," Nolan whispered.

"What now?"

"We wait for breakfast. Ozzie and Harriet promised juice and rolls, remember?"

Seconds crawled into minutes. Minutes slogged toward an hour. He could sense her trembling next to him. He fought the tightness his body wanted him to suffer.

Good Morning America came on—that made it eight o'clock. They had been untied for over two hours, and still Nolan hadn't found a way to check Mr. and Mrs. Nolan out of this dump!

Then a click at the door signaled unlocking. The knob turned. Ozzie pushed the door open before retrieving from the sidewalk just outside a tray with four juice boxes with straws, kid-style. Half a dozen small frosted rolls rested directly on the tray, on no dish or plate of any kind. Ozzie was apparently making his first stop here, bringing enough orange juice and rolls for Bud and Lou, too.

"Rise and shine, boys and girls," Ozzie said with a big dopey smile. He was in a light blue sweater today and a yellow shirt with tan khakis. His white butch hair stood up like he'd seen a ghost in an old cartoon.

Nolan said nothing. Sherry, too. The couple just looked at him with quiet contempt.

"Harriet apologizes for the rolls," Ozzie said, coming around on Nolan's side of the bed first. "It's those darned refrigerator things. She's been feeling poorly or you'd have been treated to some of the finest pastries this side of Denmark."

Ozzie was right next to Nolan now, tray extended to allow his guest to bring his bound hands up and make his selections. But Nolan's ropes fell away as he thrust his right hand out and selected instead the .45 Colt pistol in Ozzie's waistband.

"Set it down," Nolan whispered. "To one side."

Ozzie did that, though a few juice boxes and rolls tumbled off in the process. The Mushroom Motel's host smiled a big fat nervous smile and held up his hands, Nolan already off the bed and in his face, shoving the barrel of the .45 in its owner's belly.

Whispering harshly, Nolan said, "Call for Bud and Lou. Don't sound the alarm—just get them in here."

Ozzie swallowed. Nodded. Then called out, nice and natural, "Hey, Lou! Hey, Bud! Could use a little help here."

"Good," Nolan whispered.

Lou ambled in first, a Colt .38 automatic in hand but at his side, and then Bud, who had a big nasty Colt Python .357 in his mitt, also pointed down.

Nolan shot the fat little man in the head, splashing blood and brains behind him onto Bud, who panicked and turned tail and scrambled back through the hole without even trying to get off a shot.

Nolan was about to pursue Bud when Ozzie grabbed Nolan's arm, trying to wrest the .45 back into its rightful hands. Nolan shoved him aside and, irritated, shot him in the head, too. Ozzie's feet came out from under him and he went down on his back, with a *whump*, as if a rug had been pulled out from under him.

This barely registered on Nolan, who was already ducking through the hole into the next room, where track-suited Bud was sprinting through its meager furnishings—no beds, just a recliner and a couch—heading for the door. Nolan shot and missed, and the tall thug half-turned and returned fire, prompting Nolan to duck behind the end of the threadbare couch.

Then, staying low, Nolan peeked around and caught Bud with a slug in the back of the head, just as he'd reached the door, which Bud slid down, a smear of red following him to the floor, where he looked as if he'd had the sudden urge for a nap. A long fucking nap.

When Nolan stepped back inside their room, he found Sherry kneeling over Lou, taking the dead man's .38 automatic from his limp fingers.

"Good girl," he said.

"He died so quick," she said, looking up with wide eyes, her face ashen, the big gun overwhelming her rather delicate hand.

"Head shots'll do that."

The door opened and Harriet was standing there with a double barreled shotgun in her frail-looking hands—gray hair askew, no *Baby Jane* makeup yet, just a witch swimming in a floral print dress, legs in hosiery that hung loose like skin a snake was shedding. The gun seemed bigger than she was.

Then Harriet's eyes found her husband dead on the floor and she banshee-screamed, in pain, in misery, in rage, pausing momentarily to swing the shotgun's black-eyed barrels from Sherry to Nolan, trying to decide who to kill first.

But before Harriet could choose, Sherry from her low angle fired Lou's gun at the woman, the bullet going in under the chin and erupting in bloody puzzle pieces that would never be assembled into anything that made sense.

Sherry screamed.

Harriet's weapon fell first, tumbling from her hands and landing with a clunk. Then, like a tent whose poles had given way, she fell to the floor, a bony corpse lost in the fabric of the floral dress.

Sherry scrambled to her feet and into Nolan's arms, the scream a momentary lapse not followed by tears. She held onto him and didn't see him nod to the dead woman, part of whose brain showed and some of her skull, too, bits and pieces of both scattered nearby.

"Yeah," he said to Sherry. "Head shot stops 'em cold."

He held her there as he considered prowling the entire hotel, to make sure no one was around he didn't know about. But getting out of here seemed a higher priority.

Sherry stayed right with him as he checked out the sparse quarters that Bud and Lou had inhabited on guard duty—besides the few pieces of secondhand-store furniture, there was a mini-fridge and a microwave. On a coffee table he found keys to that vintage red Thunderbird out front.

"Listen," he told Sherry. "Go around and find anything either of us might've touched and wipe off fingerprints. Like those Coke bottles, for example. I'll do the same with the guns we used."

She did that while he staged the scene, leaving all of the bodies but Harriet's where they were. He wanted it to look like somebody had raided the motel, so he turned Ozzie's wife around and moved her deeper into the room, to avoid making it seem that she'd been in the doorway (which of course she had). He gave Ozzie the unfired shotgun. He let Bud and Lou have their own guns. If any of those had been licensed by the deceased, that would help make this appear as if they'd been invaded and fought back.

Before long the two survivors were standing outside where only an occasional car was going by on Highway 95. They looked like they'd had a very hard night—Nolan, unshaven, in his rumpled brown Armani suit, Sherry, hair mussed, in her torn and wrinkled black cocktail dress, neither wearing shoes.

Nolan, who had Ozzie's .45 Colt automatic in his waistband, decided on borrowing the vintage red-trimmed-white Thunderbird. The other option was the pickup truck that surely belonged to the late Ozzie and Harriet, and that seemed better off left here. He assumed the history of the place was known to at least certain members of the Vegas PD and the Clark County sheriff's department. So a raid here by men with guns wouldn't be a surprise, even if its exact purpose remained unknown. Once back in Vegas, Nolan would have to dump the Thunderbird, which presumably belonged to Bud and/or Lou. Kind of a pity. Sweet ride.

He slipped an arm around Sherry's shoulders. "Well, I think that's it. Want to check the office for Mushroom Motel postcards?"

She managed a laugh. "No. If they're vintage, I might get radiation poisoning."

They were heading for the Thunderbird when they noticed a car coming north on Highway 95. The vehicle slowed—a sand-colored Taurus that all but blended with the desert—and pulled in, stirring a little gravel-dust cloud. Nolan moved in front of Sherry and put his hand on the butt of the .45 in his waistband.

Harry Bellows hopped out on the driver's side and came around. He had an automatic in his hand, possibly a nine mil or another .45, held down at his side. His expression seemed concerned.

"Nolan!" he blurted. "I got wind of what happened. Are you all right?"

The rider was getting on out, too—Vin, the white-haired security prick from the French Quarter. He had a gun in hand, too, a snub-nosed revolver, also at his side. He smiled and nodded, which told Nolan a lot.

"I'm fine," Nolan said, and shot Harry in the head, leaving a fine mist of red when the casino exec flopped onto the gravel on his back with his shattered skull spilling out much of its contents. Vin, startled, started to bring his gun up but Nolan fired at him and took off a chunk of his left ear. Vin yowled and clutched at the bloody results.

"Back inside," Nolan said to Sherry, and she did as she was told. The "obey" part again.

Vin was running. Away from the car, heading down the row of motel rooms, maybe planning to duck into one, possibly just to get around the building where he'd have some cover. He was nearing the empty swimming pool now. Having missed the bastard's head once, Nolan went for a larger target and put two in Vin's back, the thunder cracks of the reports sounding hollow in the dome that was the desert sky.

Vin, at the edge of the pool, tottered, as if maybe one of his feet might still work, when neither really did, and then he made an unintentional, graceless dive into the deep end.

Nolan jogged to the pool's edge and peeked carefully over. The white-haired Vin lay on his back on a bed of tumbleweed and refuse, as if he were floating on water that wasn't there, his eyes staring up at nothing.

Though the man was obviously dead, Nolan—on the off-chance Vin might be faking—added a bullet in the head to the mix.

"All clear!" he called, and Sherry came out, ashen again.

As he walked back toward her, a kick from the rear of Harry's car got his attention. Then a muffled voice came from within the Taurus trunk.

"Nolan!" the voice was saying, over and over, interspersed with, "Let me the fuck out of here!"

He smiled to himself. The voice was familiar.

After popping the trunk, Nolan looked in at a wild-eyed Jon, curled up like an oversize fetus. Along the side of his head, the younger man's hair was matted with dried blood, fresh enough not to have turned brown yet.

"You're okay!" Jon blurted, overjoyed.

"Never better," Nolan said.

He gave Jon a hand and helped him out.

Sherry was heading over, looking not unhappy to be getting out of the company of the corpses inside, even though she had to step around another on the gravel apron.

"*You're* okay, too!" Jon said to her.

"That may be overstating it," she said, and paused alongside the Taurus. "There's a briefcase in the back seat."

Nolan peeked in—a dark brown hard-shell briefcase. He said to Jon, "Check Harry's pockets for a key."

Jon, who after his uncomfortable ride stretched a little and cracked his neck, noticed Harry on the ground staring sightlessly at the sky.

"I heard the gunfire," Jon said. "Is that who you shot?"

"One of them."

Jon went over and bent near Harry and started going through his pockets, as routinely as if checking a pay phone coin return for forgotten change. "Is the other one that Vin guy? Because he pistol-whipped me."

"His pistol-whipping days are over," Nolan said. "I think he did the same to me back at the French Quarter. Three fuckers in black stocking masks with guns are who dragged us out here. We've been held here since last night."

"Who was holding you?" Jon said, checking another pocket.

Nolan nodded toward the motel. "Four more dead in there. Keeping us on ice for Harry, I think."

"You seem pretty sure of that, since you killed him."

"I might not have if Vin hadn't smiled at me." Nolan shrugged. "What Harry had in mind, I'm not sure."

"Harry was there when I got taken," Jon said. "Pretty sure he set it up." Then he came over and held out a small copper key. "Could this be it?"

"Let's see," Nolan said, shrugged, then opened the back door of the Taurus. He reached in for the briefcase, turned it toward him and the key indeed worked. When he lifted the lid, banded stacks of twenties, fifties and hundreds looked back at him.

Nolan's eyebrows went up. "Well."

Jon leaned in. Sherry, too.

"Fuck a duck," Jon said.

"That's a lot of money," she said.

"Hundreds of thousands," Nolan said, and shut it back up, without re-locking it. On the floor was a canvas bag with nothing in it. He left the bag but hauled out the briefcase, and handed it to Sherry, who hugged it to her.

Nolan said to Jon, "Let's dump Harry in the pool with Vin before somebody curious comes bopping along."

"Sure," Jon said.

They each took an arm and dragged Harry across the gravel and then rolled him into the pool. He landed next to Vin, but face-down.

Then they got into the Thunderbird using the keys Nolan found in Bud and Lou's room. Nolan drove, Sherry took the passenger seat and Jon climbed in back with the briefcase. Nolan swung out onto the highway and headed toward Vegas.

Nolan caught Jon's eyes in the rearview mirror. "Tell me what happened this morning."

Jon did, then asked, "Any idea what this is all about?"

"I think so. But first count the money. It's all banded—shouldn't take long."

It didn't, but Jon was breathless anyway. "I'm glad you two are sitting down."

"How much?" Nolan asked.

"Just over seven hundred thousand dollars."

Nolan reacted as if Jon had told him what time it was. "That explains it," he said.

Sherry, eyes popping, said, "Does it? Would you care to let the rest of us in on your thinking?"

"Harry is just the sort of guy the casino would trust to run the skim. Judging by the amount, it was a once-a-month run. Vin being along makes sense, too—as a bodyguard to Harry and protector of the money."

Sherry was frowning skeptically. "Quite a leap you're making there, Big Boy."

"Not really. Harry ran the skim at another casino, downtown, some years ago. He wasn't getting any younger—and now he's not getting any older—and was in a job that was a step down from where he'd been, with no future ahead except getting put out to pasture. So I can see him looking for a way to get his hands on just one fat month's worth of skim. Instant retirement fund."

Jon was nodding. "And you turned up at the French Quarter casing the place, and suddenly Harry and his pal Vin had themselves a handy fall guy."

Sherry said, "Now he's quoting *The Maltese Falcon*."

"He's not wrong," Nolan told her. "I don't know how exactly they planned to stage it, but it was some kind of robbery with Harry and Vin playing the victims, and yours truly, yes, taking the fall."

"But why grab *me*?" Jon asked.

"Let's start with Sherry and me being found dead at the motel with an empty briefcase. Harry would've stowed the skim somewhere on the car, maybe in the spare tire—it would fit. Or in that canvas bag and leave it somewhere safe. That much cash in those denominations doesn't take up the space you might think, and weighs only twenty-five pounds or so."

"It is kind of surprising," Jon admitted.

Nolan caught Jon's eyes in the rear-view mirror again. "Then you came along looking for me, and, speaking of fall guys, became the thief who betrayed the other two thieves—who would've been found dead on the roadside where some other betraying associate left your ass. Found with the empty briefcase and the gun that killed Sherry and me. Is my guess."

Jon's eyes were wide. "Sounds like a hell of a guess."

Sherry was frowning. "But what do we do with this?" She jerked a thumb back at the briefcase.

Nolan shrugged.

But he was smiling.

12.

A Nevada Highway Patrol Officer who enjoyed a good relationship with the casino called the French Quarter's office and asked to speak to the executive manager, personally. That request, Briggs knew all too well, was unusual.

This had been just before eleven A.M., and the casino manager had barely hung up when the phone rang again on his direct line, the one that circumvented the hotel switchboard and even his secretary. The call was from their courier at the airport in Tonopah.

"The delivery," a monotone voice told Briggs over the phone, "is an hour late. Something wrong on your end?"

"Get back to you," Briggs said and hung up.

Now, forty-five minutes later, he was at the Mushroom Motel, assessing a scene of carnage, and the only thing that pleased him about the situation was the lack of any police or deputies. The Highway Patrol officer had kept the lid on nicely.

Nothing identified Briggs as an employee of the French Quarter, much less its executive manager. He wore a dark brown polo (no logo) and lighter brown chinos and hush puppies; he might have been a tourist. With him from casino security was Leo Willis, an African American who had served in Vietnam before working in Baltimore as a cop. Big, brawny Leo was similarly dressed with only the colors—gold polo and purple slacks—to hint at him being a French Quarter employee; he had a .38 revolver on his hip, however, which meant he wouldn't be confused for a tourist.

Briggs and Leo took a tour of the corpses and the two rooms

that contained them. The room next to the motel office had been set up for watchdog duty, and one of those watchdogs—who Leo identified as a low-level, off-the-books debt collector nicknamed Bud—was dead on the floor near the door. Probably trying to escape. The gun in his hand, a .357 Colt revolver, had apparently done him no good.

Leo, who was wearing latex gloves, knelt and took the gun from limp fingers and sniffed the barrel. "Recently fired," he said.

Briggs gestured toward an ancient couch where a bullet had clearly struck, stuffing pluming. "This is probably what he hit."

In the next room the body count climbed—another leg-breaker, a chubby one nicknamed Lou, lay on his back with a bullet in the head; the husband and wife who had run the run-down motel, whose only client was the French Quarter, lay dead, the woman on her back with a big hole in the top of her skull and her feet toward the door, no weapon, the man sprawled between the bed and the bathroom, a shotgun beside him—unfired, Leo said.

"It smells like an outhouse in here," Briggs commented, wincing.

"At least one of 'em," Leo said, "evacuated."

"Somebody left?"

"No. Evacuated as in shit themselves when they died. Happens a lot."

Briggs shuddered, just a little. "Remind me to eat light before I'm murdered."

Leo, who had no discernible sense of humor, just flashed him a mildly confused look, then asked, "What the hell you think happened here, Mr. Briggs?"

"Not sure. Robbery maybe."

"No skim in that Taurus. So robbery for sure, I'd say."

"Right. But who perpetrated it? Is the question."

The Highway Patrol officer stuck his head in the door. He was about thirty-five, tan and handsome, his silver-lensed sunglasses and gray-blue uniform with silver buttons as sharp as he was corrupt.

"Something you should see out here, Mr. Briggs," the officer said.

Briggs went out with Leo trailing, and followed the officer to the edge of the swimming pool at the far end of the low-slung, paint-peeling building, past the parking lot.

"Don't know how I missed this," the officer said.

The three men looked down at the two corpses, one face up, the other face down on a bed of scrubby leaves and garbage and sand.

"That's Vin," Leo said, pointing at the face-up victim, not terribly regretfully though he'd often worked with the man.

"Don't have to turn the other one over," Briggs said, nodding at the big head and small feet on the whale of a body, "to know that's Harry Bellows."

"I can go down there and check," Leo said, "if you like, sir."

"No." He turned to the officer. "Are we good?"

"Nothing here to attract attention, Mr. Briggs. Nothing suspicious visible from the highway."

"We'll get a clean-up crew out here straight away," Briggs said. He turned to his security man. "Use the phone in the car."

"Yes, sir."

Leo trotted off.

The officer said, "My chief says tourists used to come stay here and get up early to watch the atomic tests. Gawk and grin at the mushroom clouds, chief says."

"I heard that."

"Some crazy shit."

It was ambiguous as to whether the officer meant watching mushroom clouds or the nearby rooms full of slaughter.

"Very," Briggs said. "The two running this place may have got off easy."

"How so?"

"Think of the chemo bills they were spared."

The officer had nothing to say to that.

Leo came back and said, "On their way."

Briggs walked Leo over to the car, a light blue BMW, also minus a French Quarter logo. He said to his security man, "Stay out here and supervise. Call my office for a ride back."

"Yes, sir."

Briggs nodded and was getting into the car when Leo came over and said, "Sir?"

"Yes?"

"Something odd in there."

"Oh, really?"

"Well, we're supposed to think this was a straight-up heist. Like maybe Bellows and Vin got forced off the highway into this little parking lot and killed for the skim. And then some people inside, that the crew didn't expect, got mixed up in it and guns started going off."

Briggs grunted. "And then, what? The action was out here and, after, the bodies got moved inside? To keep this from getting noticed immediately?"

"Maybe."

"That's not what the crime scene says."

Leo's eyes tightened; he was the ex-cop, but the boss always knows best. "What *does* it say, Mr. Briggs?"

"You saw those duct tape strips on the floor? Makeshift gags, maybe? The roping that was chewed up here and there? Someone was being held."

The African American frowned. "And got rescued?"

Briggs sighed. "I don't know. I really don't."

Leo's expression grew thoughtful. "Was this that fella from yesterday, you think? That thief that Chicago said we should lay off of 'cause he was a Family 'friend'?"

"Nolan." That had occurred to him long ago, but he nodded. "Maybe. Either he was planning this from jump, or he put it together partly out of spite, after we gave him a hard time the other day. But nothing about this really fits together right."

Leo gestured toward the swimming pool. "Bellows was a friend of this Nolan dude. Went *way* back with him. Could be they was in it together. Could be Nolan crossed him, and...I don't know, Mr. Briggs. Only thing I do know is something weird sure as shit went down here."

"Something did," Briggs agreed. "But if Nolan had any part of this, I can guarantee you one thing, Leo."

"Yeah?"

"Our associates in Chicago will be displeased with their 'friend' Mr. Nolan."

Leo having chauffeured him out here, Briggs drove himself back to the casino. On the twentieth floor, he called security and asked them to check on the Nolan party in the Honeymoon Suite in the overflow facility, and to let him know immediately if they were there. If not, the suite was to be staked out to see if Nolan returned.

Finally, the casino manager gave his security chief a description of Nolan and said to report to him, directly, if the man was seen anywhere on the property.

Then Briggs called the Tonopah airport number and had the courier paged.

"There's been an interruption," Briggs told him.

The monotone came back: "A serious interruption?"

"A rude one. We're looking into it."

"So no delivery today?"

"Possibly not. Send my apologies and my assurance that we're on it."

"I would suggest you make another call."

Fucking disrespectful asshole.

"I will," Briggs said, "but I need to look into this first. Before I have more to say."

Briggs hung up.

He glanced at the photos on his desk in his expansive, walnut-and-ebony office. His lovely wife Karen and his two boys, Jason and Brian, beamed at him from various frames. Celebrities posing with him, both show business and political, grinned supportively from his wall of fame. His life of country club, Chamber, Kiwanis, and Guardian Angel Cathedral could not be more respectable. And yet today he'd stood in a shabby ghost of a desert motel in the company of corpses who had shit themselves.

The phone rang and it was his security chief.

"Sir, the suite appears to be vacated."

An echo of *evacuation* reverberated in his brain.

Briggs asked, "Has the Nolan party checked out?"

"No, sir. And I will let you know at once if there are any reports of Mr. Nolan on site."

"Thank you."

Shit! The bastard was in the wind.

He thumbed his Rolodex for the number. *The* number. He stared at it. How did you tell someone that the $700,000 they are expecting has disappeared? Has been taken? You can speak of your suspicions about Nolan, who happens to be someone they trust and who they vouched for, meaning you would be seeming to shift the blame to them....

Fuck.

He reached for the phone and it rang and he jumped a little. The security chief again.

"Sir, he may actually be on the property."

"*May* be?"

"If he is, he's making no secret of it. He's in the casino."

"Gambling?"

"No, uh…having a beignet and a cup of coffee. In the Lagniappe Café."

Briggs sat up. "I want two of our best muscle boys watching from across the way. If he makes *any* move that strikes them as suspicious, they are to weigh in. But they're to be discreet about it—make sure they stay out of sight unless they're needed."

"Yes, sir."

Briggs got up, threw a cream-color sports jacket on and headed out so quickly it startled both his secretary and the outer-office receptionist. He cut like a keen knife blade through the casino, that world of no clocks and no windows, where weather was something abstract, of slots spinning and dinging and donging, as the patter of dealers and croupiers lulled their prey into just one more bet.

The café was in sight.

It was him all right.

Nolan.

Sitting at the little white metal table behind the white wrought-iron railing, sipping coffee. He wore a French Quarter baseball cap and matching t-shirt, black jeans and sneakers. The son of a bitch could not have looked more relaxed.

Next to him on the floor, up against the table legs, was a brown hard-shell briefcase.

Briggs approached the café, nodded to Nolan, who nodded back, got himself a cup of coffee, and settled in at the other of two seats at the round-topped table.

"Mr. Nolan."

"Mr. Briggs."

"Would you like to explain yourself?"

The mouth smiled just enough to lift the mustache. "Perhaps *you* would. I'm hoping you can convince me you had nothing to do with my abduction."

Briggs almost blurted that last word back at him, but then some pieces slid in place.

The casino man said, quietly, establishing a low-key tone for the conversation, "You were abducted."

Nolan nodded. "And my wife of two days. By one of your security people. Vin. I didn't catch his last name, but he was in league with Harry Bellows."

"I thought Harry was a friend of yours."

"I thought so, too. You're never too old to learn. You've been out to the Mushroom Motel this morning?"

"I have."

"Interesting place. Do you suppose Ozzie and Harriet glowed in the dark?"

"Neither was aglow when I saw them."

"No. I would guess not."

"What happened out there, Mr. Nolan?"

"I can tell you what I know."

Which he did, a harrowing tale of his wife and himself being sapped and stuffed in a panel truck and driven to a motel in the desert and thrown onto a piss-stained mattress, bound and gagged. Of spending hours working free from ropes on wrists by utilizing a rusty spring as a cutting tool, and fighting back in a melee that involved the deaths of the captors, and then of Bellows and Vin who had arranged the captivity.

"Quite a yarn," Briggs said. "But *why* were you held?"

Nolan's shrug was slow and elaborate. "Several scenarios come to mind, but they all involve Bellows and his crony stealing the casino's seven hundred thousand dollars, and me taking the blame."

"…You know the amount of the missing funds."

"I do."

"Would you mind sharing those scenarios?"

Nolan opened a hand. "Not at all. But would you mind refilling my coffee for me? I'm keeping an eye on those two gents you have watching me, or us. They can do remarkable things with steroids these days, can't they?"

Briggs had spotted them, too. Stay out of sight, he'd said. But he'd neglected to mention they shouldn't wear the casino staffer's standard purple suit and gold shirt.

"You haven't touched yours," Nolan said, nodding toward the casino man's coffee. "Might be cold. Have them warm it up."

Briggs collected both cups of coffee. He brought back fresh ones and sat. Nolan put some cream in his. Briggs took his black.

"Something you don't know," Nolan said, after sipping the coffee, "is that Harry and Vin also snatched a friend of mine. Young fella employed here, actually. Plays keyboards in the Showroom combo."

Briggs frowned. "Jon's his name?"

"Jon's his name, yes. They pistol-whipped him, too, and stuffed him in the trunk of that Taurus. I don't know precisely what Harry had in mind. But I think he planned to kill me and my wife and my friend Jon, making us seem to be the parties who helped themselves to the monthly skim."

"You're guessing."

"Educated guess. Harry was in a desperate place. He wanted to get his money-grubbing cutie-pie wife back, and he resented that you had him down here playing glorified floorwalker when he was running casinos while you were still playing grab-ass at frat-house toga parties. That's how I figure Harry saw it, anyway. We both know he was over the hill, and hardly qualified to run an operation of this size."

Briggs sipped his coffee, which was as hot as this customer was cool. "You believe Harry capable of killing all those people—you, your wife, your friend, the four at the Mushroom…?"

"Not sure. But he was sure as hell capable of having Vin do it. And I would bet…if I were a betting man…that Harry intended to kill Vin, himself, to make the robbery appear more convincing …and to have the whole seven hundred thousand to himself."

"That number again."

"That number again. But don't get attached to it."

Briggs frowned. "What's that supposed to mean?"

Nolan held up a palm. "I'm getting something under the table. If your bully boys head over here, hold them back, would you?"

Nolan reached under the table. The bully boys started over. Briggs held up his hand. Nolan set the briefcase on the circle of white metal.

"Have a peek," Nolan said. "It's unlocked."

Briggs turned the briefcase toward him and unsnapped the latches and looked in. Green banded bills looked back at him. He shut the case.

"You're returning this," Briggs said.

"That's not how I'd put it."

"How would you put it?"

Nolan shrugged one shoulder. "I recovered it from the scene of a robbery that I fucked up for some people of yours who betrayed you. That's how I'd put it."

Briggs smiled, chuckled. "Are you expecting a reward?"

"I wouldn't want to put you to that trouble. So I've taken care of it myself." He nodded toward the briefcase. "That's shy twenty percent. Call it a finder's fee."

Briggs felt a flush of irritation, but then he thought about it.

Then the casino manager said, "I will admit that you were in-convenienced...but not by me. And not by the French Quarter. In fact, it's the casino that was inconvenienced."

"The casino was inconvenienced," Nolan admitted, nodding. "But not by me. And if I had not been there to handle these murdering bastards, you would have lost the skim...and, if Harry had gotten away with his scheme, you'd have plenty of explaining to do to our mutual Family friends in Chicago."

Briggs thought some more. Then: "We're talking $140,000."

"Which is a lot less than your end—$560,000."

"*Our* end? That money *is* ours, all of it."

Nolan shrugged. "Price of doing business. I suggest you keep this embarrassment to yourself, and go ahead and get the monthly skim delivered today."

"Without the missing twenty percent?"

"Who's to say it's missing? I know how the skim works. It's no set amount. You're just taking a little off the top."

"Skim the skim?"

"Skim the skim."

Briggs thought about it.

Then he began to laugh and laugh and laugh.

Finally he reached across the table and shook Nolan's hand.

The casino manager rose, gripping the briefcase handle. "You wouldn't be interested in a job, would you?"

"No thanks. I have my own set-up. But that's generous."

They strolled out of the café together.

Briggs said, "You and your wife want to stay a few extra days, just let me know."

"No, we head home Sunday." He snugged the baseball cap down and, heading off, said, "I think we've done Vegas."

13.

The compactly muscular blond young man—a black UNLV windbreaker over his vintage "Keep On Truckin' " t-shirt—was playing video poker for quarters without paying much attention. Chiefly Jon was keeping watch on Nolan during the meeting with Briggs, the executive manager of the French Quarter.

Right off, he spotted the two security guys, both of whom he'd seen around but whose names he didn't know, who also were standing vigil on the meet. Or anyway sitting vigil—the two bruisers were in Crawdaddy's at the bar having beer for breakfast.

Well, Jon thought, *there are plenty of cereal grains in beer, so why not?*

He was at a machine midway between the Nolan/Briggs confab and the two security thugs in the bistro across from the coffee shop, both of which were open onto the casino floor.

All Jon knew about the two watchers was that he'd seen them now and then, showing up when some muscle was needed, although they were hardly alone in that department. Casino goers were mostly well-behaved, but when somebody had to go, they went, and quick. Like yesterday morning, when two others of the breed had shuffled a guy as formidable as Nolan off to be given the third degree.

Of course, these two were obviously not used to surveillance duty, or they might have worn something besides the standard purple of the casino's male staffers. But it made Jon's job easy, even if he was uneasy carrying it out. He had a .38 snubbie in his right windbreaker pocket, and in Jon's mind that lump of steel was about as hard to miss as a cheerleader's camel toe.

The only glitch in his own surveillance duties happened when he hit four sevens, and quarters came clattering into the payout tray. Not wanting to take time to cash them in for folding money, much less fill his pockets with coins, he started betting the five-quarter limit. His winnings dwindled to nothing by the time Nolan and Briggs were on their feet shaking hands, with the casino man lugging that hard-shell briefcase in his other hand.

Nolan waited for Briggs to disappear before exiting the café. Jon waited for the two security boys to either follow Nolan or tag after the casino manager. Or maybe they'd just have another glass of breakfast. But soon they gave up their post to head off in the same direction as their boss.

Jon caught up with Nolan just outside the casino.

"The clowns in purple and gold?" Nolan asked. He hardly looked like himself in a casino baseball cap and t-shirt.

"Trailed after Briggs. I think we're cool."

"Unless somebody else got a call on a walkie."

Nolan walked toward where Jon had parked the Mustang convertible in the front lot. Jon fell in with him.

Jon said, "Looked like your talk ended up friendly."

"Yeah. I think it did."

Jon drove—it was his car, after all—and Nolan kept his eyes on the rear-view mirror. The trip to the shabby apartment complex and Jon's second floor pad took ten minutes.

Sherry was waiting inside. Moments after they entered, she got coffee for everyone. Three piles of money, banded $20, $50 and $100, were on the table as if being served up as a breakfast more appetizing than beer.

They all sat. It was like a poker game without cards. Jon removed the snubnose .38 from the windbreaker and rested it on the table, slinging the jacket behind him over his chair. Nolan had his long-barreled revolver in front of him. Only Sherry, in a blue jumpsuit, was unarmed. She showed no signs of what she'd been through, though her blonde-tipped hair was uncharacteristically back in a ponytail and she wore no makeup.

Nolan told Sherry, "The casino guy went for it."

"You thought he would," she said with a tiny smile.

Her husband shrugged. "He's better off just making this go away, and not look bad to his bosses, than coming after chicken-shit money like this."

She laughed and nodded at the piles of green. "*This* is chicken-shit money?"

"To them it is. Not that they wouldn't kill you over it."

Nodding to the cash, Jon said, "Why three piles?"

"Because," Nolan said, "Sherry deserves a cut, too."

"Of course she does," Jon said, hurt a little that Nolan had misunderstood. "But *I* don't."

Sherry touched Jon's hand. Just a hint of a certain attraction between them flickered in her blue eyes. She said, "You do deserve it. We insist. You came looking for us and got kidnapped for your trouble."

"And sapped," Nolan said, "like I did. Your share is $45,000. Our collective take is $95,000—our shares are a little more than yours, but we had extra pain and suffering."

Jon laughed. "No argument. Any advice?"

Nolan slid the stack of green toward him. "Buy the comic book shop in cash from the guy. Keep some paper saying he sold it over to you for a grand or something. Put the rest in a safe deposit box and spend it gradually. You know the drill—play things close to the vest."

Sherry said to Jon, "The casino's aware we're friendly. They could be watching."

"I been in this town long enough," Jon said, looking at the pile of money in front of him, "to know to keep my hole card covered."

Nolan gestured to the nearby living room with Jon's drawing

board where a page of *Space Pirates*, black ink on white Bristol board, was in progress; the furniture looked random, movies and comics posters littered the walls—it was a dorm room outfitted at a Goodwill store. Jon knew that was what Nolan was thinking.

"Keep living like this for a year," Nolan said. "If you could stand it this long, you can stomach it a while longer."

"I don't mind living like this," Jon said, a little defensive.

"Would you object to living better? Maybe a climate-controlled room for your funny books, and a wall-size TV to watch old movies on?"

"That wouldn't suck," Jon admitted.

"Maybe you could even find a woman worth living with."

Jon shrugged and he and Sherry exchanged glances. "It's possible, I suppose. But I'm like you, Nolan. I'm picky."

"Well," Nolan said, "you'll want to wait till you have that comic book shop up and running and making some income before you start living better."

Jon frowned. "They know they paid us off, Nolan. Why hide spending it?"

"They don't know you were part of it. Yes, they realize we have history. But what happened at the motel, they don't have any idea you were any big part of that. So let's leave it that way. And, of course, you want to keep the IRS at bay. Those fuckers are thieves."

That made Jon smile, and Sherry, too, although Nolan didn't seem to find anything funny about it.

"So what now?" Jon asked. "Straight to the airport?"

Nolan shook his head. "No. We're flying out tomorrow, on the tickets our late buddy Harry Bellows arranged, with our winnings in our suitcase." He put his hand on Sherry's, and said to Jon, "We're still on our honeymoon, remember?"

Jon blinked. "You're staying on for another night?"

"Why not? Do we want to be seen by the casino as running home, like we did something wrong? No, we're friends, the French Quarter and the Nolans. Anyway..." He checked his wristwatch. "I have tee time at Painted Desert with some yokels I took money from at poker yesterday, anxious to lose to me at golf. Sherry has her tan to work on. And we have that concert tonight."

"Okay," Jon said with a smile and a shrug.

That evening in the Creole Showroom lobby, Jon again met up with Nolan and Sherry. Mrs. Nolan looked lovely in her leopard-print dress and Nolan spiffy in a Satanic red sports jacket and black shirt and slacks. They put Jon's shiny shirt and baggy pants from GadZooks to shame.

"That makes a statement," Jon said, nodding at the bright jacket.

"And that doesn't?" Nolan said, nodding at Jon's wardrobe. "Sherry bought it for me."

Sherry, hugging her husband's arm, said, "At Fashion Show Mall. When he wears it, it'll remind him of our honeymoon."

Jon said, "Why, was there a chance you'd forget it? You should've brought home some Mushroom Motel stationery."

In the showroom, the trio settled into their front-row seats as the Everlys tore through one hit after another—"Bye Bye, Love," "All I Have to Do Is Dream," "Cathy's Clown" and so many others.

But before the duo did "Devoted to You," the brothers— who smiled and pointed when they recognized the newly married couple in the front row—coaxed Nolan and Sherry into standing and taking a bow, to enthusiastic applause. Who didn't like a honeymooning couple? And what man wouldn't have envied that lucky old hardcase with his trophy wife?

But to Jon—who retained a sentimental streak despite his

detour into a life of crime—seeing Nolan take that bow signi-
fied the end of an era, and a farewell to everything he and the
older man had done together over the years, good and bad.

At the couple's insistence, Jon joined them for dinner at the
Prime Rib Room. They feasted and talked and reminisced.
Some of what they laughed about would have seemed inappro-
priate to average folks, but these were not average folks.

Nolan got the check, saying, "You took the short end of the
cut. Least we can do."

Jon noted the "we," another indication of the era's end—it
wasn't Nolan and Jon, anymore. It was Nolan and his wife.

As the trio was leaving the restaurant, Jon said, "You were
wrong about one thing, Nolan."

"What's that?"

"We did have one last job. And it worked out fine."

Then Nolan nodded and stuck out his big, gnarly mitt in a
rare gesture between these two.

They shook hands.

Jon headed for the parking lot, thinking, *Now they can get
back to the heartland and a life where no one is trying to kill
them.*

THREE

14.

Nolan and Sherry were in Moline by just before noon. Collecting their suitcase at the modest airport took only fifteen minutes, and within half an hour they were having a quiet lunch at Harold's on the Rock, which was a favorite of theirs, and an easy stop on the way home. The A-frame restaurant, with its funky nautical touches and grounds rife with gardens and gazebos, made a pleasant setting for a luncheon back in the Quad Cities.

Sherry was having lobster and Nolan a rare filet. When the check came, he told her, "You're not a cheap date."

They were underdressed among an after-church crowd, her in a pink pants suit, him in a gray polo and black jeans. Even so, they were a handsome and vaguely mysterious couple and got looks even in a restaurant where they were frequent diners.

"Neither are you," she said. "But we did save money staying at the Mushroom Motel."

He twitched a smile at her. "We *made* money. So. Where do you want to take your real honeymoon?"

"*Our* honeymoon. Not Europe. How about Acapulco?"

"All right. Cancun's the coming thing, though."

She shrugged and sipped her coffee. "I'm an old-fashioned girl."

He touched her hand. "You want to wait till fall? It's hurricane season now."

"When did a little danger ever stop you?"

By just after two, Nolan was easing the silver Trans Am into the drive. Then he got the suitcase out of the trunk and he and

Sherry went up the sidewalk and the couple of steps to the stoop.

He asked her, "You want to be carried across the threshold?"

"And throw an old man's back out? Not interested."

They laughed and he opened the door for her; she slipped inside and turned off the alarm on the keypad at right. When he stepped in with the suitcase, before he even set it down, or had yet to shut the door behind him, he smelled it.

The cigarette smoke.

So did Sherry, who was turning to him with a frown. Neither of them smoked, and Sherry sent guests to the patio to do so. Someone had been in the house.

Or still was.

Raising a hand of caution to her, Nolan put the suitcase down, knelt and snapped it open, and dug out the .38 revolver wrapped in dirty clothes. He rose and what he whispered in her ear were not sweet nothings.

He said, "Go outside."

She began to protest, but with his free hand he squeezed her shoulder, gently, but squeezed it.

"The .25 in the glove compartment," he whispered. "Get it."

She nodded; she knew about the little Colt auto he kept tucked in there.

"You hear shots," he told her, still sotto voce, "wait to see if I come out." He began moving deeper into the house. "If someone else does, kill him."

Her smile and nod were small but terrible and he liked them very much.

Sherry slipped outside, shutting the door almost soundlessly.

Nolan prowled the house, stopping frequently to listen for anything that wasn't a clock ticking or an appliance humming or the central air purring (he'd left it on at Sherry's insistence).

Nothing.

Taking his time, gun at the ready, like a cop clearing a house after a shooting, he included closets in his search, looking not just for an intruder who might have snugged himself away on hearing them come home, but for any sign that expensive clothing items had been taken.

No evidence of either. And on first look, nothing of value had been taken from the house itself.

In the kitchen, somebody might have helped himself to a few beers, but Nolan couldn't be sure. He didn't keep track of such things. Maybe Sherry would know, but he wasn't about to bring her in for a homemaker's inventory until he knew the house was safe.

Before going down the hallway to bedrooms and bathroom, he decided to first take the stairs to the lower floor, figuring the finished basement was an ideal place for an intruder to lie in wait—to take a shot at someone coming down that open stairway and making a target of himself.

And now he moved quickly, taking two steps at a time, landing low, in crouch, fanning the revolver around.

No sign of anyone. More smoke smell, though. That told him two things: Whoever had invaded had (a) stayed a while, and (b) was a real dipshit. Who would be that dumb? Even the fucking Comforts knew the basics of criminal conduct.

Yet the lower floor—including the unfinished area with the washer and dryer and furnace and fuse box—held no surprises. Before heading back upstairs, though, he realized he'd become a target again, and took it slow, staying low, almost in a crouch, following the long barrel of his .38 all the way as if it were a divining rod.

When he reached the top, Nolan rolled and came up in a sitting position with the .38 poised to do damage, moving in a half-circle to take on anyone waiting.

No one was.

Or at least seemed to be.

Nolan rose slowly, then started down the hall. All three bed-rooms and their closets, and even under the beds, gave up no intruder. The master bedroom smelled most strongly of cigarette smoke—thinking that might mean a thief had entered and taken his time looting here, Nolan checked the dresser. Nothing appeared to be missing. A floor safe in the closet had either not been discovered or got ignored, because Nolan's stash of getaway money was still present within.

So far the only evidence of a gate-crasher was the pervasive cigarette smell, but that spoke volumes. That and maybe a few missing bottles of Coors. He'd finished his search of the bed-room and the john, when he returned to the latter to take a pee. As he was doing that he noticed the matchbook on the floor.

So.

Their guest, who had smoked in this non-smoker's house, had left further proof of his visit. Nolan flushed and knelt and retrieved the matchbook, which was from the Starlite Motel. He smiled to himself and pocketed the incriminating item.

Outside, after slinging on a light jacket to conceal the .38 stuffed rather uncomfortably in his waistband, he told Sherry it was safe to go in.

"But keep that .25 handy," he said.

She nodded. "Are you putting the car away?"

"No. I'll be gone a while. I'm following up on a lead to our visitor."

Nolan showed her the matchbook.

"Could be a local," she said, studying the Starlite logo. "An employee maybe. Or somebody and a friend checked in for an afternoon delight."

He shrugged. "Or an out-of-towner."

Her expression grew troubled. "Could the casino have sent somebody to take you out on your home turf, away from theirs?"

"Possible. But I don't think so. That executive, Briggs, is no mob guy. He's mobbed up, but not one of them. No, I think that's behind us."

"But what's in front of us?"

"I'll find out." He gave his bride a kiss on the forehead and shooed her inside.

She was clearly worried and even a little irritated at being patronized. But it was better for her to be irritated with him than dead.

Nolan was about to get in the Trans Am when the droning roar of a power lawn mower cut off and a male voice called out, "*Hey! Neighbor!* Got a second?"

Nolan turned and made himself smile and yelled, "Sure!"

He started to move toward the yard across the way and down the street a bit; but the homeowner was trotting over, so Nolan stopped and waited.

Will Beckey had been a high school athlete a couple of decades ago, and still had the look, although he was bald on top and wore glasses, sunglasses at the moment. He was in a navy t-shirt with a gold Augustana Vikings logo and shorts and sneakers, with grass flecking his ankles.

"Heard you got hitched," Beckey said, fists on his waist like Superman, even if the glasses made him more Clark Kent.

Shit, he didn't need this.

"Yeah," Nolan said, making a grin. "Finally did the deed."

"Well, you're a lucky man."

"I am. Maybe you can explain why Sally puts up with you." That was her name, right? Sally?

"God only knows," Will said. "Like the Beach Boys say."

"Yeah. Beach Boys. Good to be back." Nolan smiled, nodded, and started to turn away.

But Will moved closer—into what Sherry would call his "personal space"—and said, "Thought I better mention…a car, kinda light blue, a Dodge? Dart, I think?"

Nolan frowned. "What car?"

"While you were gone, I saw it driving around here, coming in and going around the cul-de-sac, maybe three or four times, on different days, once at night. Might be my imagination, but I thought he was slowing down when he passed your place."

"That right?"

"I mean, you're on the corner, so anybody who turns in slows down, and anybody leaving our little neighborhood, to wait for a break in traffic, well, they're gonna slow down too, so…I'm probably just borrowing trouble."

"I appreciate you pointing it out."

Will shrugged. "This is a quiet little street. We don't even have any houses for sale to attract anybody right now. It's unusual, that's all. Better safe than silly."

Nolan managed to chuckle at that. "You didn't happen to catch the license plate, did you?"

"Not the number, but it was a Missouri plate, if that means anything."

It might.

"No," Nolan said, shaking his head, "not a thing, I'm afraid. But thanks for the alert."

"Thought I better let you know. It's not like we have neighborhood watch or anything." Will grinned and waved and trotted back off.

Not wanting to alarm Sherry any more than he already had, Nolan decided to keep this to himself for now—that and a certain suspicion that was pricking the back of his neck.

In under ten minutes, he was at the front desk of the Starlite. The office was small—no part of the motel had seen a remodel since it opened around 1960—and everything was blond wood and yellow wallpaper and racks of things-to-do-in-the-QCs brochures.

The skinny balding acned dude in dark-rimmed glasses behind the counter wore a black clip-on tie that went well with his white short-sleeved shirt, black slacks and name tag, identifying him as GERALD. He was slouched in a desk chair watching a TV perched high on the wall opposite, hospital-room style. The Cubs were playing the Cardinals. This guy may have loved the game, but he had obviously been the kid who got picked last when sides were chosen up at recess.

"No vacancies," Gerald said in a whiny midrange pitch, not looking at Nolan. "Sign's hard to read in daylight, but…no vacancies."

Nolan turned the register around and had a look. "You have two Smiths staying with you, Gerald."

The crowd cheered on the tube.

The clerk said with a smirk, "Yeah. Don't think they're related."

"One is named Daniel Smith. His car's license, it says here, is Missouri."

The clerk frowned over at him. "Please don't handle that. That's motel business."

The umpire yelled, *"Strike one!"*

"My apologies," Nolan said. He got out several bills from his wallet and held one up, a five, then cleared his throat and got the clerk's attention again. "Gerald, do you give out information about your guests for a consideration?"

"Strike two!"

"Not a five-dollar consideration I don't."

"Ball!"

"How about a ten-dollar consideration?"

"Ball!"

"I don't think so."

Nolan tried again. "Maybe a twenty?"

A crack of the bat and the crowd went wild. Gerald turned the sound down with his remote, got out of his chair and came over, leaning across the counter. His breath was the result of a conspiracy between fast food and belching.

"How can I help you, sir?"

Nolan held up the twenty, folded lengthwise, between thumb and middle finger. "What kind of car is Daniel Smith from Missouri driving?"

"A Dodge Dart. Blue. Not dark blue."

Gerald reached for the bill. Nolan pulled it back.

"What room is Daniel Smith from Missouri in?"

"Second floor around back, number 27. His parking stall is numbered—painted big on the cement. I'm throwin' that in extra."

"Appreciate it."

Gerald reached again for the twenty but Nolan shook his head again. "Is he in his room?"

"That's a definite no. I saw him pull out around noon. I think that's enough bang for your buck."

Nolan gave the clerk the twenty.

"Anything else I can help you with, sir?"

Nolan opened his wallet again, got out another twenty, and held the bill up. "It's a shame you have no vacancies. But I wonder if I could take a look at one of your rooms? As a point of future reference."

"Any room in particular, sir?"

"Gerald, I understand Daniel Smith from Missouri's room is typical. And since he's out, we wouldn't be disturbing him. Might I have a quick look?"

The clerk's eyes tightened behind the lenses of his dark-rimmed glasses—Nolan had gone too far. "I'm alone here, sir. Afraid I can't accompany you."

Nolan waved the twenty gently. "I assure you I can be trusted."

The clerk thought about that, then rustled around in a drawer and came back with a room key marked 27. Held it out and made a trade for the twenty.

As Nolan exited the office, the sound on the TV came back up and the crowd was cheering again.

Walking around in back of the place, he confirmed that the parking slot was indeed boldly marked 27 in big red numbers, and was empty. He took exterior stairs up to a railed landing and within seconds was inside number 27.

The room had been made up and its occupant was no slob—suitcase on a stand, a paperback of *The Tommyknockers* book-marked at his bedside, his toiletries neatly arranged in the bathroom. Otherwise the accommodations were as anonymous as they had been before Daniel Smith checked in.

But one oddity stuck out.

Or, really, two.

On the dresser, next to the 21-inch portable TV, was a rather attractive, lidded, brown woven basket, fairly good-size—big enough to carry a bowling ball and still have room for the shoes. Nolan was taking a closer look when he noticed the other oddity—a machete.

About thirteen inches long with a typically broad, barely tapered blade.

Nolan didn't touch either object, but he studied them.

Stared at them, asking himself the question, *What the hell are* these *fuckers for?* He asked himself that several times.

In Daniel Smith's suitcase, Nolan found only fairly casual clothes, but they were mostly dark-hued. Nothing that would stand out at night. A suit whose label said CHESS KING didn't quite go along with the rest of the conservative apparel. Nolan had figured he might come across a weapon, but no such luck.

Then he found a box of .22 cartridges. Not a full box, either.

So Daniel Smith from Missouri probably was carrying a loaded .22 with him right now.

Nolan settled in a chair by the door, thinking. He did that for a while. Should he stay here and wait for the guest in number twenty-seven to return? And deal with this right here?

But the idea of handling whatever this was—in a second-floor room at the Starlite, along a main drag, with God knew how many people around—did not appeal. The opportunity to be seen and/or heard was too great. And he'd interacted with that clerk, Gerald. Nolan was a man who liked maintaining as much control as possible in this chaotic world, and this was the opposite of that. Anyway, he'd had enough fun in motel rooms lately.

He returned to the office. The ball game was still on, but the clerk immediately turned it down and got up and scurried over to the man who'd been handing out money.

But all Nolan did was say, "Here you go," plunking the key to 27 on the counter. He was heading out when Gerald spoke.

"Would you be interested in another twenty dollars' worth?"

Nolan turned.

Returned.

"Possibly," he said.

The clerk jerked a thumb toward a little switchboard back there. "All calls made from the rooms come through the desk.

We charge for calls, you see. If I'm here, I take them, and do the billing. But whoever's on duty does the same."

"Did Daniel Smith make any calls?"

The clerk folded his arms, lifted his chin. "Might have. Might've been long-distance. Might've been to two numbers only."

"…Ten bucks buy those numbers?"

"Ten apiece would."

Nolan got another twenty out, but also a ten. He gave both to the clerk. "That's twenty for the numbers, Gerald. And another ten for your selective amnesia."

"I think I get your drift."

"I think you do, too, Gerald. Ever hear of the little man who wasn't there? I'm his big brother."

The clerk smiled at that, but somewhat nervously, because Nolan had put just a hint of threat into it.

A few minutes later, Nolan pulled his Trans Am into the same convenience store lot as Daniel Clifford né Comfort the night before, though of course Nolan didn't know that. He went to the counter and got change for a twenty.

At the pay phone near the restrooms, he called home.

"Yes," Sherry said.

"Me," Nolan said. "Everything all right there?"

"Fine."

"I'm going to ask again. If someone's there with you, say 'Fine' again."

"Nolan, everything's cool. Nothing on this end, except the damn smoke smell. I've been spraying air freshener till my poor little finger hurts."

"Okay. Listen carefully. You need to leave the house. Pack a bag and take the Vegas cash with you and the .25, too. Drive your Nissan across the river and check into the Blackhawk

Hotel under your maiden name. Stay there till you hear from me."

Alarm colored her voice now. "What's going on?"

"Don't know yet. If you don't hear from me by this time tomorrow, call Will Beckey across the street and have him check the house. He's a hunter. Have him bring a gun."

"Nolan!"

"Sherry, whatever's going on, I'm ahead of it. Trust me on this. Getting you out of harm's way is just a precaution. But I think we've learned not to take things lightly."

"Nolan, I love you."

"I know you do," he said, and hung up.

He looked at the slip of paper with the phone numbers Gerald had written down for him. One was 314 area code—St. Louis. The other was 573—that covered Columbia and Jefferson City.

He dialed the 314 number, then fed coins in when the operator told him to.

On the third ring, a young-sounding, breathy female voice said, "Clifford residence."

Nolan took a shot. "May I speak to Daniel please?"

"He's not here right now. He's out of town on business, I'm afraid."

You shouldn't share that kind of information over the phone, honey, he thought, *if your looks stack up with that voice.*

Nolan asked, "When do you expect him back?"

"Dan wasn't absolutely sure, but he thought tomorrow. You know how business is."

"I do," he said. "You've been very helpful. Thank you."

Goodbyes were exchanged and Nolan hung up.

Could Daniel Clifford be a hit man? With a contract on Nolan? But what the hell would he be doing with a basket and a machete?

Nolan dialed the 573 number, dropped more coins in at the operator's bidding, and it took eight rings before his call got answered. He had almost hung up.

But then he heard an aged female voice, with an odd edge to it, say, "Mabel Comfort speaking."

"Wrong number," Nolan said, and hung up.

15.

A little after two A.M. on Monday morning, Daniel Clifford began what was in many respects a replay of his first visit to the ranch-style house in the small, upscale housing development off 16th Street in Moline, Illinois.

He again parked one street over, but tucked into an alley this time, and left the basket and machete in the parked Dart on the passenger seat. Rather than carry those items in a grocery bag, as he had on the last two visits, Daniel preferred—now that he knew Nolan and his new wife were back in the Cities— to concentrate on taking care of the pair before dealing with Maw's need for a trophy.

What the youngest Comfort brother needed was his wits about him. Nolan was, even when taken unawares, a hardass who had apparently even gotten the best of brother Cole, who was after all one vicious son of a bitch. That Daniel must enter the house undetected, corner the couple in their bedroom, and dispatch the woman before disabling Nolan, was a dizzying prospect. Every time it played out in his mind, the part where he wounded and incapacitated Nolan refused to come to life. It stayed abstract, even absurd....

So before tending to Maw's grotesque request, Daniel would concentrate on the first orders of business—remove the woman, and clip Nolan's wings before forcing from him the answer to the key question: *What happened to Cole?*

Wasn't that enough to do?

Afterward, he could return for the basket and perform Maw's grisly collection instructions, though that was the other step he couldn't quite visualize. So he had stopped trying.

But at least this time around, Daniel *knew* Nolan and the girl were back from their Vegas jaunt. He had been there to greet them, in a way, going to the Moline airport and blending in with others on hand to greet loved ones and friends arriving home from their journeys. No risk to it—Nolan had never met or even seen Daniel. And vice versa being true, he'd decided to take the opportunity to get an in-person sizing-up look at them.

He had hoped that Nolan would just seem like a man to him, a human being like Daniel with assorted frailties like any member of the species...only that hadn't been the case. Nolan looked like that actor in the Italian westerns—not Eastwood, but the mustached, narrow-eyed one. Dangerous, deadly. A devil in human form, which that casual summer attire didn't diminish a whit. The wife was a beauty, curvy and pretty and self-confident.

He felt so out of league, compared to them.

But he could almost hear his Maw saying, *They bleed and die like everybody else. Don't be afraid, boy. Don't be a fool. You're a Comfort.*

Daniel followed the couple to the riverbank restaurant where he'd dined that first night after making it to Moline. The eatery was crowded, and sitting alone in a corner at a tiny table made him feel conspicuous. But the honeymooners didn't spot him. He might have been invisible. And this made him smile to himself. He might appear to be an insignificant mustached little man with thinning hair. But he knew something they didn't, didn't he?

He was in town to kill them.

This knowledge built his confidence, strengthened his resolve. He didn't even puke up his meal this time.

After lunch, Daniel followed them home and saw the silver Trans Am turn into the housing development and then pull into the driveway. He drove on, not slowing, not giving himself away even a little bit.

Returning to the Starlite, he called his mother and told her that Nolan and the girl were finally back from Vegas and that tonight would be the night. He intended to drive straight to her place after the deed had been done and deliver her prize. Maw had, for once, sounded proud of him.

That afternoon he again tooled over to the Milan Cinemas and bought a ticket for one film—*Poltergeist III*—which he watched before sneaking into a second—*Friday the 13th Part VII*. A double feature like that required him stepping out into the lobby several times to smoke, and once to pee. He had popcorn and a Coke and Milk Duds and kept it all down. The horror movies didn't scare him at all, and he didn't jump once. Excitement was building in him.

Daniel returned to the Starlite Motel and called home and Heather talked dirty to him and he came gloriously into a warm moist washcloth. Marriage was wonderful. Heather was worth everything he was going through, and that privileged pair in their expensive rambling ranch-style digs were just going to have to sacrifice their happiness for the sake of the Cliffords.

After a post-orgasm Kent, he was even able to catch a nap, though he first called the desk and asked for a one A.M. wake-up call. And when that call came, he showered and shaved and shat, as if preparing for a night out with his honey back home, everything but aftershave. He got into the windbreaker, navy polo and matching khakis he'd worn that first night, a night he was now viewing as a dress rehearsal.

When he approached the house, the Trans Am was still in the drive, a quarter moon providing more illumination than previous visits. Again, no lights were on in the house. He checked for any signs of off-hours activity in the nearby houses, and found they were as dark and silent as this one.

But when he peeked into the double garage through its row of eye-level windows, he was taken aback by the absence of the Nissan ZX.

Why was the wife's car gone?

Was that significant? If so, why exactly?

Troubled but not dissuaded, he headed around the house, down the sloping lawn, to the patio. Again, he used the lock picks, and was soon inside. The alarm had not been set, which seemed to confirm that the man of the house was almost certainly at home this time, even if his wife wasn't—Cole's notes made it clear Nolan did not set the alarm when one or both were at home.

Again, Daniel held the silenced .22 automatic in his right hand and the little flashlight in his left. Yet even without it, he might have navigated the finished basement in this darkness, as he was now used to the layout—the pool table, the bar, the TV area, the open stairway. The latter he went up slowly, switching off the flash. On the off chance Nolan had somehow got on to him, and was up there waiting, he would not tip his presence.

But as he searched the rest of the house, with the bright narrow beam clicked back on, he established fairly quickly that the place was empty. The master bedroom had not been slept in. The guest rooms also had their beds made. Closets held nothing but clothes. And the john was unoccupied, too—the shower stall empty.

When he panned the flash around the good-size bathroom, Daniel caught sight of something that initially did not grab his attention. Then he frowned and returned the beam to a small object on the counter by the sink.

A Starlite Motel matchbook.

At first all that got from him was a confused frown looking back at him in the bathroom mirror; but then he stared at the thing, agape. He realized with sudden clarity that he'd left the matchbook in the house, on one of his visits, and that Nolan had found it.

And now the king of this castle had left it out for Daniel to see, to let the intruder know that he was busted.

Panicking now, his confidence shattered like a dropped china cup, Daniel rushed out of the bathroom and moved fast, following his flashlight beam back up the hall and over to the stairs and then down them, hoping if he was quick enough Nolan wouldn't jump out at him like Jason in *Friday the 13th*, no matter which number.

But if that did happen, Daniel was ready—he had the silenced .22 tight in his hand, arm pulled back with his inner forearm resting on his torso so that the gun couldn't be easily swatted from his grip. He barreled down the stairs into the darkness of the finished basement, almost but not quite losing his balance, terrified that flowers of orange gunfire might blossom out of the blackness.

And when he slipped out into the night, shutting the glass door but not bothering to re-lock it, the world strikingly warmer than the air-conditioned inside, Daniel did a semi-pirouette, in case Nolan was waiting, the prey now become the hunter.

But nothing happened.

And the only sounds were crickets, night birds, and the occasional traffic on the thoroughfare nearby. That and his own heavy breathing, heavier even than it had been when Heather was encouraging him over the phone earlier.

On the way back to the car, gun still in hand but in his windbreaker pocket now, flashlight tucked away too, he made himself walk slowly, or at least held back from running—he did not wish to call attention to himself. And no car slowed, not even a police cruiser that spooked him.

That matchbook, that goddamn matchbook.

It had told Nolan where Daniel was staying. At the motel the bastard could have found out about the long-distance calls. Some of the calls had been to Heather at home, the others to Maw—*how much might Nolan have figured out?*

He got quickly into the Dodge Dart, tossing the silenced .22 onto the seat next to the basket and blade, got the car started, pulled out and swung left in an opening in traffic, heading toward 3rd Avenue, where he could catch I-74 over to Iowa.

As he headed down the 16th Street hill, through a mixed commercial and residential area, he would glance every so often into his rearview mirror, with such frequency that he almost rear-ended other drivers twice. The lights of a car behind him, seeming to stay right with him, might be Nolan taking pursuit.

That seemed at once ridiculously paranoid and all too real a possibility.

When the car neared him, Daniel could see it wasn't a Trans Am at all, but a Buick Regal. And the driver was bald with glasses and certainly not Nolan.

Another car was behind the Buick, though, and it might be a Pontiac, it had those kinds of lines and shone under the street lights.

When Daniel cut over on a side street to start weaving his way over to 3rd, the Buick didn't make the turn, which flushed him with relief; but then the other car came along for the ride. Daniel, still impulsively checking the rearview, saw that this was a Pontiac, all right, a Firebird. He picked up his pace, as best he could, hitting stop signs every few blocks, then he realized the Firebird wasn't silver, but a metallic blue. And a woman was driving, heavyset and older, not Nolan's bride.

His fucking imagination was fueling the paranoia.

Calming himself, Daniel crossed the westbound bridge over the Mississippi and halfway across, for the first time in as long as a minute, he checked the rearview mirror again, breathed a sigh, then a few moments later, did it again and almost threw on his brakes.

Nolan was sitting back there.

Arms folded, all in black, a big long-barreled revolver in his right hand, just kind of casually draped.

"Eyes on the road, Daniel," he said calmly.

"What the fuck!" the driver said. "Nolan! How do you know my name?"

"How do you know mine?...Take River Drive to Davenport. That's the way you were heading, anyway, right? Going back to St. Louis, but taking the Iowa side."

Daniel kept looking at the calm face in the rearview mirror, angular features wearing unsettling shadows. "It was the matchbook. It was the fucking matchbook!"

Nolan's nod was barely perceptible. "That and the smoking. My house smells like a bar before closing, thanks to you. Don't you know smoking kills you?"

"How did you know what my car looked like?"

"A neighbor saw you. You're not exactly subtle, Daniel."

Nolan leaned up and Daniel stiffened, but his passenger was merely taking the silenced gun from the rider's seat where it had been stuffed behind the basket and machete.

"Best remove temptation," Nolan said.

They were on the downslope of the bridge.

Daniel said, "First sign of me on your property, you started looking for the car, right? Knew I wouldn't park far away."

"Right. A risk, but a small one."

Daniel swallowed. "What now?"

They had turned off the bridge onto River Drive, a brightly lit commercial area.

"Keep driving," Nolan said.

Then they were gliding along with the Mississippi at left and near-mansions to the right. The moonlight looked silver on the water. An air of timeless unreality seemed to settle over them.

As they moved past the village of East Davenport and under a railroad bridge, Daniel said, "Now what?"

Nolan said, "Straight on out. Past the downtown. Past Oscar Mayer. Then stay on 61 a while."

Daniel was almost crying, hands gripping the wheel. "What... what do you *want* from me?"

Nolan's voice could not have been more matter of fact. "I want the whole story. I know your last name's Clifford, but your real one is Comfort. I don't see much resemblance, but I'm guessing you're Cole and Sam's brother. Last Comfort standing... except for Mabel. Never met the lady, but she seems to know me. Of me, anyway."

Daniel's words came quick: "This was her idea. I didn't want any part of it. She *made* me."

Nolan's face in the rearview frowned. "What are you, twelve?"

He was shaking his head. "No...no, I needed the money. Maw has a lot of cash stashed in that house. Doesn't believe in banks. Shoe boxes, jars, canisters. She paid me to...to do this."

"To do what, exactly?"

Daniel didn't answer that, not directly. "She said if I didn't do what she wanted, I was out of the will. That she'd leave everything to Pat Robertson and some goddamn chapel that makes cutesy kid figurines. And I need money *now*."

"Tell me, Daniel." Nolan's tone was strangely unthreatening, as if, despite his fearsome features, he was sympathetic.

It all spilled out. The loans Daniel had faked, the bank examiner on the way, the old wives who wanted alimony and child support, the current wife who wanted nice things, the new house with the cost overruns. How Maw wanted Daniel to force Nolan to tell him what happened to Cole.

"Well, that's easy," Nolan said. "I killed him."

Daniel frowned uncomprehendingly at the mirror. "But you and Cole were doing a *job* together! How could you kill one of your own crew?"

"Oh, it was no double-cross, Daniel. Cole blackmailed me into helping him pull a heist in my own back yard. Made me shit where I eat, which I don't find appetizing."

Daniel knew his late brother well enough to find that credible.

"Plus," Nolan went on, "he kidnapped my woman—the one I just married. I told him if he so much as mussed her hair, I'd shoot him in the head."

"What…what did he do?"

"He mussed her hair.…Make a right."

A sign said WEST LAKE PARK—TWO MILES, then added in smaller letters beneath BOATING, HIKING, FISHING, SWIM-MING. They moved through a deserted wonderland of glimmering lakes and trees reflecting ivory moonlight. Now and then there would be a turn-off.

Finally Nolan said, "Just another five minutes or so. It's the upper tip of the park.…How were you going to make me talk, Daniel?"

Daniel avoided the rearview mirror. "Just, uh…you know. Hold you at gunpoint."

An edge came into the backseat voice. "You'd have killed my wife, wouldn't you? Right there in bed where she slept. And if I woke, you'd've put a couple of non-fatal rounds into me, to handle me better.…right?"

"*No!* No, never. Just…"

"Right. Like you said. Just hold me at gunpoint and I'd tell you everything…and then what?"

Daniel said nothing.

"Kill me," Nolan said flatly. "You couldn't leave me alive. And I'm guessing your 'Maw' doesn't have a forgiving nature."

"She doesn't," Daniel admitted. He let himself look at Nolan in the mirror again, and once more the words came fast: "What if I told her you were dead? And went in the house and kept her talking and you sneaked in? And killed her. Wouldn't be hard. She's an old woman with a walker. Do it quick so it doesn't hurt. Then we go treasure hunting and split the money."

"Kill your mother."

Daniel raged at the mirror. "She's a monster! She's a witch! Do you know what she wanted me to—" He stopped himself.

Nolan smiled at the driver in the rearview. "Cut off my head? Put it in that pretty basket? Deliver it to her like flowers and a box of Russell Stover?"

Daniel said nothing.

The area on the northwest corner of the park was densely wooded off to the right. A graveled apron gave access to a trio of picnic tables, beyond which—starting up without preamble—a narrow gravel service road led into the woods. At night, not a soul was around.

"Pull in here," Nolan said.

"Why?"

"It's what your mother wanted."

"What is?"

"I'm going to show you where your brother is buried."

16.

Mabel Winifred Comfort—Maw to those who knew and loved her, or anyway knew her—was in a particularly fine mood on this sunny Monday morning in June.

On Friday, an associate in the fencing operation had provided to-and-from transport to Curl Up & Dye in Jefferson City, to get her hair fixed, and now her skull cap of permed gray curls looked almost nice enough to be a wig. On Saturday, the colored girl had been in to clean, and the interior of the old farmhouse was spic and span, every velvet painting straightened, shag carpeting swept, the clear vinyl covers on the living room furniture fairly shining from their damp-cloth wipe-down.

The smell of lasagna cooking in the oven in the now spotless kitchen was pleasantly permeating the downstairs—Daniel's childhood favorite. Her secret was combining one pound of sweet Italian sausage and three-quarters pound of lean ground beef, and really hitting the garlic hard. No Hungry Man TV dinner for her boy today! All she had left to do was set the table—the little Negro gal from town had already cleared the counters, filling cabinets with clean dishes and Hefty bags with garbage.

The meal would be ready by noon. She figured Daniel would be here by then. For the first time in forever, she was looking forward to seeing him.

Yesterday, when they'd talked on the phone, Daniel had told her, "They're back in their house. So I'm going to do it tonight."

"Good. Good."

"Maw, can we skip the one part?"

"What part?"

He didn't answer, not directly. He just said, "That basket is very pretty. Shame to waste it. I could just give it to Heather and she could fill it with flowers and make a centerpiece out of it."

"No! You want your Maw to bail you out of the mess you're in, you be a good boy and *please* her!"

"...Okay."

"Be strong, son. I know waitin' around while those two are off in Vegas playing hide the salami hasn't been easy. But patience is a virtue, the Good Book says."

"I'm not sure that's in the Bible, Maw."

"Well, it should be! Don't you be afraid. You're showing yourself to be a real Comfort. What you been doin' shows spine and what you're gonna do'll show the world you got balls as big as your brothers."

"Thank you, Maw."

She'd kept the pep talk up a while, then the call was over, and she wound up feeling more sure of the boy than ever before. Sure, he had his doubts; sure, he had some shivers. But Daniel had rolled with the punches and was prepared to do what she said, like a good son.

Last night, she'd had trouble getting to sleep, just thinking about it. She was fixated on finally getting some closure where Cole was concerned—she was as convinced her middle boy was dead as she could be, short of actually knowing.

Now she would.

And Nolan would suffer before he died, which was the cherry on the sundae. He would see the woman he loved in bed next to him, shot to shit, and he would be wounded painfully to keep him in line while the truth about Cole got squeezed out of him.

She wished she could be there.

That was why she needed her trophy. She wanted to see that

man d-e-a-d *dead*. If she still had a garden, which she didn't, she would put that bastard's fucking head on a pike to scare off the crows. But she figured she'd just wait till it began to stink and bury it out back somewhere.

The other thing that had kept her awake was unexpected: a sense of pride for her youngest son. She knew damn well this experience would be the best thing in the world for him. That he would come back stronger, of mind and stomach and testicle, and he would at last be back in the fold.

She began to fantasize—but a fantasy she felt could be realized—that Daniel would walk away from that straight-ass city job and join her here in the country. She wasn't going to live forever, after all, and Daniel would have earned the right to sit by her side, and learn the ways of the trade, and take over when she was gone.

As for that little slut of his, Heather, well, she'd be welcome, too. Maw figured to give the girl the upstairs to do with what she wanted. And if the couple wanted to build their own place, as fancy as the one they put up in St. Lou that got them in financial difficulties, why, that was fine, too. Maybe Daniel could knock the bitch up and give Maw some fresh grandkids to help raise right. Give them a real sense of family pride.

These thoughts had kept her up last night—must have been almost half an hour before she finally got to sleep—but she hadn't slept in, this morning. No. She had showered and got freshened up and powdered and everything, and into her best floral muumuu, big pastel blossoms that looked like Hawaii, or anyway made her think of the only Hawaii she knew, the one in that Elvis movie.

Getting antsy, she used the walker to get herself into the living room, where she plopped into the recliner and watched Home Shopping for a while. Suzanne Somers was selling her

ThighMaster for $19.95 plus postage and handling. Maw would have to order one of those when some new stolen credit cards came in.

As noon approached, Maw and her walker trundled out to the kitchen, where she set the table for two using the new cute kitties plastic placemats she ordered out of the Fingerhut Christmas catalogue. From a cabinet, she selected un-chipped matching plates and glass tumblers just right to pour beer in. She wanted this almost…elegant.

This was a special homecoming.

Maw had the table exactly how she wanted it when she heard the stir of gravel outside. She trudged with her walker back to the living room and opened the front door. A car she didn't recognize was in the drive, a Dodge wasn't it? An in-between shade of blue. She pushed through the door out onto the stoop to where she could see in the car—but no one was in it.

Then she smiled, remembering that Daniel had mentioned that the car he'd got from Eddie's Motors in St. Lou was a Dodge, and that it had driven fine with a working air conditioner and radio and everything.

So her boy was home.

But where was he? Maybe come in the back way, through the kitchen. To surprise her. The scamp.

So she waddled back in there and saw, on the table, arranged in the middle like a centerpiece, that lidded basket she had given Daniel to fill. Her face split in a smile and she pushed her walker aside and, moving like a toddler, she took the last few steps between her and the table. Then she leaned in and, thinking what a fine son Daniel had turned out to be after all, lifted the lid from the basket she'd woven.

Daniel's eyes looked up at her. His mouth was open but no words were coming out. In the middle of his forehead was a black-crusted, slightly irregular hole. Where his neck had been cut, it was one quick clean stroke.

Maw backed away from the head in a basket, horrified, a scream curdling, and she made it all the way into the living room, without her walker, before she flopped onto her back, hitting hard enough that the nearby Duke and Elvis paintings shivered.

Gasping, she held onto the center of her chest, wadding the muumuu fabric between clutching fingers. She felt as though a blade had been thrust through her heart, and she was trying to catch her breath as she looked up at a man who seemed impossibly tall, hovering over her. He was all in black and mustached like a Mexican and he had a long-barreled revolver in his hand. His expression was impassive though he was watching her close.

Nolan, she thought.

Nearby, while the old woman was dying, the Home Shopping Network took orders for a Prayer Boy doll, a sleeping little baby sucking his thumb.

17.

You can have Las Vegas, Sherry thought. *This is the life.*

The Princess Hotel in Acapulco was a fifteen-story Aztec pyramid of a building perched on something like five hundred lushly tropical acres. The marble-floored honeymoon suite with its pale shades of yellow and green and turquoise had floor-to-ceiling glass sliding doors onto a private terrace and a view of the sparkling azure Pacific.

They had been here two days with a spa for her and two golf courses for Nolan and four restaurants for them both. As for that endless beachfront, the sand was golden, the water warm.

They were twenty minutes from a downtown teeming with dining, shopping and nightlife, and a plaza strewn with festive outdoor music. Yesterday evening they had watched a cliff-diving show that lasted till a sunset caught the ocean on fire.

Laying out mornings in the skimpiest of white bikinis, Sherry was careful not to burn, already halfway through a bottle of Coppertone; she could hardly even detect its salty, orange-blossom scent from the ocean air anymore.

She had never been around so many other foxy young women in bikinis, but she didn't feel particularly intimidated. Afternoons, like right now, she stretched on a beach-style lounge chair beneath an umbrella near the pool, in white short shorts and matching tank top; she wore ivory-rimmed sunglasses as she read a paperback edition of *Presumed Innocent* by Scott Turow.

Nolan, also in sunglasses but wire-rimmed, in black swim trunks and a lightweight short black robe, ambled over from his trip to the poolside Bamboo Hut Bar. His body was just hairy enough and his scars added a sense of life having been lived. He came bearing zombies. He handed her one and she sipped it as he settled into the lounge beach chair beside her.

She said, "You ever going to tell me?"

"Tell you what?"

"What happened that night."

He sipped his zombie. "What night?"

"The night you sent me away and dealt with our smoker."

"No."

"Not even where all that money came from?"

When he'd summoned her home roughly twenty-four hours after packing her off to a room at the Blackhawk, she came in to find the kitchen table covered with jars and shoe boxes and canisters and what have you, all brimming with money—cash, no coin. Mostly twenties or higher. It was the damnedest thing.

"If I told you," he said, "you might think less of me."

"Why is that?"

"Maybe I scared an old woman to death and stuck around to loot her premises, before her body was even cold. But money is money."

She chuckled. "Right. *That's* what you did."

"Not the worst of it. But if you knew, you'd be party to it, and I like you innocent." He nodded toward the book fanned open on her lap.

"Well," she said, and sipped her zombie, "I'll give you one thing, Mr. Nolan."

"What's that, Mrs. Nolan?"

"You do know how to show a girl a good time."

Some young fool cannonballed into the pool and got gleeful screams from pretty, nearly naked females frolicking.

"I try," he said.

WANT MORE NOLAN?

Read the Whole Nolan Series By
MAX ALLAN COLLINS
Coming Soon From HARD CASE CRIME!

Two For the Money

Nolan needs one last score before retiring from a life of crime, but it all depends on the help of a green kid named Jon.

Double Down

Stealing from the criminal Comfort clan is risky enough for Nolan and Jon without an interloping skyjacker and would-be vigilante waiting in the wings.

Tough Tender

Their cover blown, Nolan and Jon must pull a job for the second time at the behest of a blackmailing bank exec and the deadly femme fatale behind him.

Mad Money

When his girlfriend is kidnapped by an old nemesis, Nolan is forced to assemble a plunder crew to heist an entire shopping mall in a single night!

Read On for the Opening of
The Book That Started It All,
TWO FOR THE MONEY!

Prologue

A woman was usually a night to a week in Nolan's life, yet this one had lasted a month and five days. But then, before it was different—before he'd never had so bad a need for one.

He sat up in bed, aware that the pain in his side was lessening, and scanned the room. He took in its drabness, and a slight smile came to his lips. Christ, had he really been staring at these four suffocating walls for over a month now? He closed his eyes, seeking not rest but relief from pink stucco walls and secondhand-store furniture.

"Hi," she said. She was in the doorway, bundled in a heavy coat, a sack of groceries filling her arms.

He nodded hello.

"I'll just put these away," she said.

He kept nodding, said, "Okay," and watched her smile and leave the doorway.

He leaned back and reached out his arms while stretching his body. The pain didn't increase at all from the movement; the place in his side where the bullet had gone in seemed completely healed over. Quite a difference from even a week before, when his body had been one big ache, one long, slow, muscle-bone-gristle ache.

He got out of bed and caught, turned away from his reflection in the bureau mirror. He climbed into a pair of boxer shorts, shaking his head and muttering.

That damn face of his, high cheekbones, narrow eyes, widow's-peaked hair, that damn easily recognizable face, which both beard past and mustache present failed to disguise. At least the lean weeks had affected his body somewhat to the better. He felt drained, sure, but that roll of softness the years had put around his waist had disappeared.

"Hi," she said, in the doorway again, now wearing only bra and panties.

She had never been beautiful, he supposed. But she'd been better than plain, and nowhere near ugly. Now, after seven or maybe eight years of traumatic experiences—assorted divorces, abortions, affairs with married men—she was getting the kind of lines in her face that polite people say show character. Nolan saw the lines as too much age for too few years, giving her an air of having been taken advantage of emotionally, used once and thrown away like Kleenex.

"You look tired," he said.

She nodded, undoing the scarf that tied her black hair behind her head, letting the shoulder-length mane fall free. "I'm tired, all right," she said, "but not physically, you know, just mentally. I mean, the old mind really gets a workout waiting tables eight till five. It's a goddamn challenge."

As she spoke, Nolan watched bitter lines deepen in her face and then lowered his eyes to her breasts as she released them from her bra. The breasts were large, and though beginning to sag, were still quite good. Her nipples were like rose-hued sand dollars.

"How was your day, Nolan?"

"Long. Dull." He went back over to the bed and lay down again.

"How's the side?" She came and stood by the bed and leaned over him, her breasts swaying like hanging fruit.

"What?"

"Your side, how's it feeling?"

"Better."

"Do anything today?"

"Just slept."

"Oh? Now don't hand me that line…you haven't been sleeping more than nine hours out of every twenty-four since you been feeling better, and you had near that when I left for work this morning. So what'd you do today?"

"I watched television."

"Sure you did. The soap operas."

"That's right."

"Come on, Nolan."

"I read the paper."

"Do anything else?"

"No."

"Took you all day to read the paper?"

"Slow reader."

"All right, so be a bastard."

"That was an accident of birth."

"Smartass remarks don't make you less a bastard, Nolan."

"Okay, okay. I suppose I ought to tell you, anyway."

"Tell me what?"

"I made a couple long-distance calls."

"You did?"

"Yeah, I'll pay for them. I'm going to pay you back for everything you've done for…"

"Shut up, Nolan." She sat down on the bed, facing away from him and touching her face with her fingertips.

"What's the matter?"

"Nothing."

"What?"

"You don't owe me a damn thing, that's all. Do you understand?" Her voice was drum tight. "I am a lot of things, and I've been a lot of things, and I will be a lot of things in days to come.

But I was not, am not, and will not ever be a whore." She was quiet for a few moments, then added, her voice hushed, "You don't owe me anything, Nolan. And if you try to give me any money, I'll tear your goddamn heart out."

He touched her shoulder.

She turned and rubbed her hand over his chest, twining her fingers in its hair. She made an effort and got a smile going and said, "I won't try to pry out of you what those phone calls were about—you don't have to worry about that."

He nodded, smiled.

"Did you do anything else today?"

"No. Just did some thinking."

"That's what I was afraid of. That's why those stupid damn phone calls put me on edge so."

"What do you mean?"

"Now you've started thinking."

"Thanks a bunch."

"You know what I mean. You've started thinking, and before I know it, well…"

"Well what?"

"Well, you'll be gone, damn it."

He didn't say anything.

"You *are* leaving," she said, "aren't you?"

"I didn't say that."

"You said you been thinking. Same difference."

"Sometime I'll leave. Everybody leaves sometime or other."

"You're half right. Everybody leaves me *all* the time."

"What is this, self-pity day?"

"You're goddamn right it is. Who else is going to pity me if I don't? You?"

"How old are you?"

"What? Why are you forever asking me how old I am?"

"Don't make me ask again."

"All right, all right, I'm thirty-one."

"What else are you? Besides thirty-one."

"Free, white, and ten years too many?"

"You're intelligent. Not bad looking."

"Beautiful is what I am. A funhouse mirror with sex."

"Shut up. You're a good-looking kid."

One side of her mouth smiled. "Maybe I should have pulled this self-pity routine before. I've never heard you talk so much —and compliments, too! Don't stop now."

He allowed himself a grin and said, "I'll grant you I don't talk much, but now I am, so listen, I got something to say: sling hash if you want to, or don't sling it."

She looked at him wide-eyed. "That's it? That's the big message?"

"That's it."

"Profound. Pretty fuckin' profound, Nolan. 'Sling hash or don't sling it.' Let me write that down."

He laughed and grabbed her arm. "Okay. You think about it. For now let's shut up and get on with it."

Her lips took on a wry smile, and she latched her thumbs in her panties and tugged them off. "You got yourself a deal."

They made love, slow, grinding love, and it was as good for them as it had always been over the past month of Nolan's recuperation. At the beginning, because his wound was serious, their lovemaking had been gentle, increasing in intensity as the weeks passed, each time different for them. Nolan was amazed that this one woman could seem to be so many different women. Never having bedded down longer than a week's time with the same woman, he had assumed a woman's sexual possibilities could be sufficiently explored in that time or less. It was a pleasant surprise to him to discover at this late date that he was wrong.

After several hours of sleep, Nolan and the girl awoke to darkness and, checking his watch, Nolan said, "It's nine, kid. What shall we do?"

"Hungry?"

"Yeah."

"What do you want?"

"How about breakfast?"

"At nine o'clock at night?"

"Yeah."

"Okay."

She climbed out of bed, slipped on her bra and panties, got into a houserobe, and went out into the kitchen.

Fifteen minutes later Nolan and the girl sat at the kitchen table, eating the evening breakfast of scrambled eggs, bacon, and toast in silence. Nolan's attention was on his plate of food, while the girl stared at him intently.

She broke the silence with, "Why do you ask me what my age is all the time?"

"Do I?"

"You did tonight, and I bet it was the hundredth time, too. Why?"

"To make a point."

"What point is that? Oh, I remember, don't remind me, that quote of yours that'll go down through the ages: 'Sling hash or don't sling it.'"

He looked up from the plate. "That's the one."

"There's got to be more to it than that."

"Maybe there is. You never bothered asking how old I was, did you?"

"No, I didn't. But then, you told me at the start not to ask you a lot of personal questions. For my own sake, you said."

"That's right. But you don't have to ask, I'll tell you. I'm forty-eight."

She was surprised. "I thought forty, maybe…but, hell, so what? I been had by older men, that's for sure."

"You never met anybody older than me. I'm a dinosaur who can't get it through his head he's extinct."

"What are you…"

"I'm forty-eight and I'm hiding out with a girl who spends her days slinging hash, and I'm living off her while I get recovered from a gunshot wound."

"You said not to ask questions, Nolan, so…"

"I know. You're not asking, I'm telling. You got time left. You got stuff left in you. I'm running out. Of time. Of stuff. I picked what I am, and I blew it. I got nothing left to do but make the best of the sucker choice I made a long time ago. Till it's over."

"I don't…don't follow you, Nolan."

"You don't have to. You got a life of shit here. Change it. Change yourself. You got time left to choose again. Me? My life's shit because I picked wrong. Too bad. Too late."

"I think you're feverish again."

"No, I'm not. Have you been listening to what I said?"

"Of course, Nolan, of course…"

"Sometime when you got nothing to do, think about it." He wiped his mouth with a napkin and got up from the table. "Let's not talk anymore. I'm tired again."

They went back to bed, fell asleep quickly, then woke in a few hours and made love, hard, fast, violently. Then Nolan and the girl rolled apart and went back to sleep.

At five the next morning the phone rang them awake, and Nolan went for it, spoke a few times and listened for a minute and a half without answering, said, "Yes," and hung up the phone. He went back to bed and pretended sleep, just as he knew the girl was pretending she hadn't seen and heard what had just happened.

At six-thirty the girl kissed Nolan on the cheek as she was preparing to leave the apartment for work. Nolan grabbed her, stroked her face, and smiled goodbye. Then he rolled back over in the bed and closed his eyes and she was gone. When she'd been away an hour, Nolan got out of bed, called the bus station to confirm his reservation, packed his bag, and left.

1

The drizzle felt good on Nolan's face. The night air was chill, though not enough to freeze the drizzle, and the light, icy sting of it on his skin kept him alert as he waited.

He was sitting on a bench in the parklike strip of ground that separated the Mississippi River from the four-lane highway running along it. The highway connected the Siamese-twin cities of Davenport and Bettendorf, whose collective reflection on the river's choppy surface vied for attention with that of Rock Island and Moline on the other side.

Across the highway was where Werner lived.

Werner's home was a white, high-faced two-story structure, nearly a mansion, complete with row of six pillars. Already bathed in light by the heavily traveled and streetlamp-lined four-lane, the house was lit on right and left by two spotlights set on either side of its huge, sloping lawn, which banked down gradually to the highway's edge. Even through the heavy mist, the whiteness of the overlit house made a stark contrast against the moonless night around it.

Typical Werner logic, Nolan thought, picking a place like that one: status plus prestige equals respectability.

Nolan had been waiting just less than an hour. His side of the road was darker, and the constant traffic flow and hazy weather seemed likely to obscure him from anybody who might be on watch over at Werner's. He hadn't seen any watchdogs yet, but he knew one would show sooner or later—a Werner-style watchdog, two-legged-with-gun variety.

He smoked cigarette number one off the first pack of the

evening, second of the day. He was pleased when the drizzle didn't put it out. Just as he was getting number two going, he spotted Werner's man.

The watchdog came around from the back, walking slowly around the house, probing the thick shrubbery on both sides of it with a long-shafted yellow-beam flash. He was slow and methodical with his search, and after the shrubs had been checked, he headed for the paved driveway to the left of the house. He stood at the far end of the drive and let the flash run down over it, then walked toward the back of the house again.

Probably a garage back there, Nolan thought, the drive leading around to it.

Three minutes later the watchdog reappeared at the right of the house and began to move slowly over the sprawling lawn, crisscrossing it half a dozen times before angling down on the highway's edge. He stood there for a moment in the light of a streetlamp, and Nolan got a look at him.

Not overly big, just a medium-sized guy, wearing a hip-length black brushed leather coat, open in front to reveal a dark conservative suit, complete with thick-knotted striped tie. The man didn't look particularly menacing, but Nolan knew he'd probably been chosen for just that reason.

Subtle muscle. Typical Werner.

Nolan's hand in his jacket pocket squeezed down around the rough handle of the .38. He put on a smile and stood up from the bench. Stepping out into the stream of traffic, sidestepping cars, Nolan called out to the watchdog.

"Hey! Hey buddy..."

The watchdog had turned to walk away, and Nolan met him about a third of the way up the sloping lawn.

"Say, I think I've gotten myself lost. You couldn't give me some directions, could you?"

The watchdog had a bored, bland face that didn't register much change between glad, sad, and indifferent, although Nolan could read it well enough to rule out glad. The hand with the flash came up and filled Nolan's face with yellow light.

Nolan squirmed and held his free hand up defensively to shield his eyes, but he kept the smile plastered on. "Look, friend, I don't want to bother you or anything, I'm just a stranger here and got my bearings fouled up and thought maybe you could…"

"This isn't an information bureau," the watchdog said. "What this is is private property. So just turn your ass around and go back across the street and take off. Any direction'll do."

The flash blinked off, and Nolan could tell he'd been dismissed.

Nolan gave him a bewildered-tourist grin, shrugged his shoulders and began to turn away. Before the turn was complete, Nolan swung the gun in hand out of his pocket and smacked the .38 flat across the watchdog's left temple. The watchdog's eyes did a slot-machine roll and Nolan caught him before he went down. Nolan drunk-walked the limp figure up the remainder of the lawn, carefully avoiding the glare of the spotlights, and took him over to the left side of the house, dumping him between two clumps of hedge. He checked the man's pockets for keys but found none. He did find a 9mm in a shoulder sling, and tossed the gun into the darkness.

Subtle moves were fine for Werner and company, but right now Nolan hadn't the time or energy for them. The watchdog would be out for half an hour or more; plenty of time. He glanced out toward the highway, which by now seemed far away, and decided that there wouldn't be any threat from some public-spirited motorist stopping to question his handling of the watchdog situation. Thank God for mist and apathy.

He walked around the house in search of an unlocked window,

trying not to let his out-in-the-open sloppiness with the watch-dog bother him. He just didn't seem to have the patience to work things out smoothly these days. Making a mental promise to tighten himself up again, he tried the last of the windows.

Locked.

Well, there might be one open on the second floor, and a drainpipe was handy, but Nolan ruled that approach out: his side, while improved, was not yet in that kind of shape, and he was beginning to think it might never be.

He broke the glass in a window around the back of the house, seeing no need for caution since the neighboring houses on both sides were blocked by stone walls, and a large three-car garage obstructed the view from behind. A light was on in a window over the garage door, probably the watchdog's quarters, explaining the absence of house keys in the man's pockets. Nolan slipped his hand in through the glass-toothed opening in the window and unlocked it. Then he pushed it up and hauled himself slowly over and into the house.

He caught his breath. The room he found himself in was dark; after stumbling into a few things, he decided it was a dining room. A trail of light beckoned him to the hall, where he followed the light to its source, the hairline opening of a door.

Nolan looked through the crack and saw a small, compact study, walled by books. Werner was sitting at his desk, reading.

Several years had passed since Nolan had last seen the man, but their passing had done little to Werner: he'd been in his early twenties for twenty-some years now. The only mark of tough years past apparent in his youthful face was a tight mouth, crow-footed at its corners. The almost girlish turned-up nose and short-cut hair, like a butch but lying down, overshadowed the firm-set mouth. His hair's still jet-black color might or might not have come out of a bottle, though Nolan felt fairly certain that the dark tan was honest, probably acquired in Miami.

A rush of air hit the back of Nolan's neck, and he started to turn, but an arm looped in under his chin and flexed tight against his Adam's apple, choking off all sound. He felt the iron finger of a revolver prod his spine as he was dragged backward, away from the cracked door.

A whisper said, "Not one peep."

The watchdog.

Shit.

"That gun in your hand," the whisper said. "Take it by two fingers and let it drop nice and gentle into your left-hand coat pocket."

Nolan followed instructions.

"Now," the whisper continued, "let's you and me turn around and walk back into the dining room, okay? Okay."

The watchdog kept his hold on Nolan's throat and walked him along, each step measured. Once they were out of the hall and into the dining room, the grip on Nolan's neck was lessened slightly, though the pressure of the gun was still insistent.

"Keep it quiet and you'll get out of here with your ass," the watchdog whispered. "I'm only going easy on you because I don't want my boss in there finding out I let somebody slip by me. A window with some busted glass I can explain, you in the house I can't. So just keep it down."

They approached the broken window through which Nolan had entered, and the watchdog released him, shoving him against the wall by the window. Enough light came in the window for the two men to make their first good appraisal of each other.

Nolan had been right about the guy being tougher than he looked. The whole upper left side of his face was showing a dark blue bruise, and a still-flowing trickle of red crossed down from his temple over his cheek, but the man's expression remained one of boredom, only now it was as though he were bored and maybe had a slight headache. He'd shed the leather topcoat, and his suit was a bit rumpled, although the striped tie was still firmly knotted and in place.

"Sonofabitch," the watchdog said, "an old man. I got taken down by an old man. Will you look at the gray hair. Sonofabitch."

Nolan said nothing.

The watchdog's upper lip curled ever so slightly; Nolan took this to be a smile. "Let's get back outside, and a younger man'll show you how it's done....Come on, out the window."

The hand with the revolver gestured toward the open window, and Nolan grabbed for the wrist and slammed the hand down against the wooden sill, once, then again, and on the third time the fingers sprang open and the gun dropped out the window. Nolan smashed his fist into the man's blackened temple, a blow with his whole body behind it. The hard little man crumpled and was out again.

Nolan leaned on the wall and gasped for breath. Half a minute went by and he was all right; his side was nagging him again, but he was all right.

He undid the watchdog's shirt collar and untied the tie, then used it to lash the man's slack wrists behind him and picked him up like a sack of grain and tossed him out the open window, where he landed in the hedge. Nolan figured he'd stay there a while longer this time around.

When he returned to the door of the study, Nolan peered in through the crack and saw Werner, undisturbed, still at his desk, reading. With the .38 in hand, Nolan drew back his foot and kicked the door open....